The Go-Between

L. P. HARTLEY

Level 4

Retold by Roland John and Judith Brown
Series Editors: Andy Hopkins and Jocelyn Potter

Pearson Education Limited
Edinburgh Gate, Harlow,
Essex CM20 2JE, England
and Associated Companies throughout the world.

ISBN: 978-1-4058-6244-8

First published in the Longman Structural Readers Series 1972
by arrangement with Hamish Hamilton Limited
This adaptation first published by Addison Wesley Longman Limited
in the Longman Fiction Series 1996
First published by Penguin Books 1999
This edition published 2008

6

Illustrations by Tim Beer

Typeset by Graphicraft Ltd, Hong Kong
Set in 11/14pt Bembo
Printed in China
SWTC/06

Published by Pearson Education Ltd

Contents

Introduction

'The messenger of the gods! I felt very proud. I was a traveller through heaven, visiting one god after another. It was like a wonderful dream – and it soon became a real dream.'

It is the summer of 1900, and Leo Colston, the main character in *The Go-Between*, is living in a dream world. He is excited and proud to be the messenger for several adults at Brandham Hall.

At almost thirteen years old, Leo has left his careful, sensible mother and his quiet, middle-class life to spend the summer holidays at the home of Marcus Maudsley. The two boys know each other from their school, but they are different types and not close friends. Marcus does not question his place in the world. He comes from a rich, upper-class family and is confident that he deserves the best of everything in life.

Leo's father is dead. He has no brothers or sisters, little money and a lower position in society. This background has produced a different kind of boy. Leo must earn his success, and he uses his imagination and intelligence to do this. He has a gift for writing magic spells, and when it appears that some of his spells work, he earns a certain level of popularity at school. This leads to an invitation to Brandham Hall, the fine home of the Maudsley family.

For Leo, Brandham Hall is not only a place where he can see how rich and powerful people live. It is also a wonderful world where he can be accepted as one of the actors, as he happily takes the job of messenger for three of the people that he meets and admires.

But not everything at Brandham Hall is as bright and beautiful as it seems at first. Leo has to grow up during this summer. Although he prefers to stay young and innocent, he has to learn about secrets and lies, and about the power of sexual relationships. This new knowledge becomes too much for Leo. He feels angry, guilty and confused. In many ways his future life has been destroyed.

Leslie Poles Hartley, the writer of this book, was born in 1895 in Cambridgeshire, England. His father studied law and later became the manager of a brick-making factory. Both parents believed in the importance of good health and hard work. Possibly because of his father and mother's strong religious views, L.P. Hartley once said that as a boy he always felt he had done something wrong.

There was enough money in the family for them to live in a large country house, which looked like a castle, and to send the boy to private schools. Before going to Harrow (one of the most famous and expensive boys' schools in the country) Leslie went to Northdown Hill School, where he especially enjoyed sports. In August 1909 he was invited by one of the other boys, Moxey, to stay with his family at Bradenham Hall in Norfolk. It seems very likely that Northdown Hill School became Southdown Hill School, Bradenham Hall became Brandham Hall, and Moxey became Maudsley in *The Go-Between*.

Hartley had a slow start at Harrow, where his background made him seem different from the other boys. This position of outsider prepared him for his life as a writer. He watched and learned so he was not laughed at. He found ways to be part of the group, and eventually he became a happy, successful schoolboy. He was captain of one of the football teams; he won a prize for the long-jump; he was very good at cricket and other sports, and he was head of the school in his final year. But he never forgot his feelings as a lonely child on the outside, looking in.

Hartley began studying Modern History at Balliol College at the University of Oxford in 1915, the second year of World War

I, and made friends with some of the most important thinkers of the day, including Aldous Huxley. But because of the war, he left Oxford in 1916. He joined the army and had several desk jobs in England, but left in 1918 because of poor health.

Hartley was shocked by the violent war and the terrible number of deaths. He believed that as a result society had lost its connection to a better, happier time. He described the past as 'a foreign country: they do things differently there'. This view of a better, sunnier time is clear in Hartley's writing, especially in *The Go-Between*.

Hartley returned to Oxford, where he continued studying until 1922. During that time he began to write for a number of magazines and continued to make friends with other writers and artists. In the summer of that year he made his first trip to Venice. He fell in love with the Italian city and returned to it regularly, except during the years of World War II. He admired the strong, handsome boatmen on Venice's waterways, and he used them, and the city, in his writings. The physical beauty of Ted Burgess, one of the main characters in *The Go-Between*, was perhaps modelled on one of these boatmen.

After Oxford, Hartley turned seriously to writing. His judgements on modern literature were welcomed because they were intelligent and fair. His own first book of fiction, *Night Fears and Other Stories*, appeared in 1924. Many of the subjects in this work were repeated in his later works: the past is seen as a simpler, better time; love is dangerous, and ordinary things may become mysterious and terrible. The book was liked by intelligent readers, but it was not a financial success.

Hartley wrote only a few works of fiction over the next twenty years, but in 1944, *The Shrimp and the Anemone* appeared. This was the first of three books about the lives of Eustace Cherrington and his sister Hilda, fictional characters who were loosely modelled on the writer and his sister Enid. Eustace, like Hartley at Oxford, meets important, rich people, but again like Hartley, he always feels like an outsider. Hartley's family earned its money from the brickworks. He was always aware of the difference between his social level and the class of many of the young men around him. In the Eustace and Hilda books, as well as in *The Go-Between*, characters suffer from the knowledge that they will never be upper class. Also, as in *The Go-Between*, there is a relationship which ends badly. In Hartley's books, happiness does not last, and he was always doubtful about love, in his writing and in his private life.

Before his death from heart problems in 1972, L.P. Hartley had written seventeen works of fiction and had won many prizes for literature. By then he was known as a rather difficult person. He entertained many guests, but he did not always like them. He drank too much and criticised modern life and working-class people. He often argued with his servants and with people he worked with. Without a wife, partner or children, he left his letters, books and documents to his younger sister, Norah. When she died in 1994, all his private papers were burned.

The Go-Between (1953) is Hartley's most famous book, and when it came out it was an immediate success. Although it is about a young boy – whose childhood is similar to Hartley's in many ways – the story is told by the boy when he is a lonely man in his sixties. On the first pages, we learn that Leo Colston has found his childhood diary from the summer of 1900. Then we watch as he re-lives the experiences of that time when he saw too much, learned too much and ran away from real life.

Hartley places the story in 1900 because he believed that it was a time when life was good and people were confident about the future. To him, there was a feeling in England of safety and happiness before World War I; everything was perfectly in its place. But in the story, Leo is out of place. He suffers at school because of his middle-class background, but he understands that world and can solve his own problems. Then he is invited to Brandham Hall and is excited about being part of the Maudsleys' upper-class life. Unfortunately he never really understands this unfamiliar world, and he never has a real position in it.

The secret relationship between Marian, from the upper class, and Ted Burgess, a farmer, is also out of place. It does not fit within the rules of the day, and in Hartley's stories physical love often causes heartbreak and even death.

Marian is Marcus's beautiful older sister. She is kind and understanding towards Leo and, like a typical schoolboy, he falls completely in love with her. He will do anything for her. Marian knows how Leo feels and asks too much of him, but at first the boy does not understand what he is doing. Marian makes Leo her messenger and brings him into her life of secrets and lies.

When Leo understands the purpose of the messages and realises that Marian has been using him, his life begins to fall to pieces. In many ways his life is ruined; he becomes a lonely adult and limits himself to facts, keeping away from love and emotions for more than fifty years. Hartley shows a great understanding of the difficulties of growing up, and also of the effect that a frightening, upsetting experience can have on a whole life.

Today L.P. Hartley is remembered for *The Go-Between*. The book was made into a successful film in 1971. As a result of both the book and the film, many people understand something about life in England in 1900; they also have a clear picture of a beautiful, dreamlike, but disastrous summer.

Chapter 1 The Diary

I found the diary by chance. It was lying with some other things in an old red box. My mother had probably put them there many years before. They were the sort of things that every boy collects. It was a pleasure to see them again. They were like children that I had not seen for more than fifty years. I couldn't remember anything about the diary. I looked at it for a long time but refused to touch it.

I picked up a lock from the box. It was a special kind of lock, with three rows of letters. If you moved the letters into the right position, the lock would open. As a child I could place the letters correctly even if my eyes were shut. This used to annoy my friends at school, who believed that I had some magic power.

The letters now moved round between my fingers, and I shut my eyes. I tried to imagine that I was a little boy at school again. Other boys were watching me. The letters moved slowly, and I felt each one. At last I found the right position. There was a faint sound, and the lock opened in my hand. At the same moment I remembered the secret of the diary.

It was a secret that frightened me. I remembered the defeat that I had suffered. The message of that diary was quite clear. It told me that my character was weak. It also told me that I had not been strong enough to solve my problems; I had failed. When I found the diary, I was sitting alone in a dusty room. My mother's old things lay around me, and I was thinking about the past.

The diary contained an account of the events which had changed my life. If those events had never happened, my life would have been different. I would probably have married and had children. My house would be a warm and bright place. My thoughts would be about the future, not the past.

I picked up the diary and opened it. On the first page I read:

The twelve star signs appeared in a circle around the words, and I knew them well. They had been important to me when I was a boy. Each sign had suggested confidence, life and power. The smaller beings in the signs were playing happily, and they stood for young things and young people. The year 1900 was the first year of a new century. I was twelve years old in 1900, and I hoped for great things in the twentieth century. The larger beings in the signs stood for the men who would rule the world. I intended to grow up to be like them.

The Virgin was the only lady in the circle. I did not know what she meant. Her long hair almost covered her, and she wore no clothes. I often thought about her, and in time she became the chief figure in the group.

It was an exciting time, and I was looking forward to the new century. 'Nineteen hundred, nineteen hundred,' I used to repeat to myself. Would I be alive on 1st January 1900? I had doubts sometimes. I had been ill the year before, and the idea of death was not strange to me. I tried to forget my fears and waited patiently for the new year.

I told my mother about some of my hopes for the future, and the diary was a present from her. She, too, hoped that 1900 would be a great year for me.

I was born on 27th July, and so the Lion was my particular star sign. I admired the Lion's strength, but he was not human. I wanted a human figure that I could try to be like. There were three in the star signs, and I chose the Virgin. I hoped that she would help me in the twentieth century.

In January 1900 I had taken the diary back to school with me. And it had had one good result immediately. I knew the star signs so well that my teachers were very pleased. But it had another, less fortunate result. It was a beautiful little book, and 1900 was a very special year. So I decided that my diary should contain only important notes. They would be written in my best English.

I tried to remember the things that I had written. I turned the pages quickly. There were reports of games between my school and another school. We had played three times against Lambton House School, and at last we beat them. In my diary I had written: 'Lambton House VANQUISHED.'

Vanquished! I remembered that word very well. I suffered because I had written it. I usually kept the diary in my desk, and I hoped to guard its secrets. But I had to let the other boys know about it because, like the lock, it gave me an advantage. Others looked up to me because I had a secret.

One day someone took the diary from my desk, and the secret was discovered. Suddenly there was a crowd of boys around me.

'Who said "vanquished"? Who said "vanquished"?' they shouted. They threw me to the ground, and a number of boys pressed on top of me.

'Are you vanquished, Colston?' someone shouted.

For a week after that they vanquished me every day. My body and my arms and legs felt sore, but I knew that the punishment was my own fault. I should not have written the word 'vanquished'.

At the same time I was anxious to prove that I had not been vanquished. The boys were afraid to keep something that had been stolen, and they put the diary back in my desk. That evening I went to a small room where I was quite alone. I cut my finger with my knife and put my pen in the blood. I wrote two magic spells in the diary.

I am looking now at those faint signs and letters. I had invented the signs, and they did not mean anything at all. But I remember the two names clearly. JENKINS and STRODE: they were the boys who attacked me most frequently. On the next page of the diary I had written:

SPELL THREE
AFTER SPELL THREE DEATH FOLLOWS
Written by my hand and in my BLOOD
THE LION

I should have been ashamed of those spells because they were wrong. But I was not ashamed of them then, and I am not ashamed of them now. I am jealous of the strength of character that I used to have. When I was young, I used to fight enemies in my own way.

After I had written those spells, I put the diary in my cupboard. It was soon discovered by the boys. They attacked me again and beat me to the ground.

'Are you vanquished, Colston, are you vanquished?' Strode shouted. 'Who's the lion now?'

Sitting across my shoulders, he pressed his fingers under my eyes. It was a terrible experience.

That night, in bed, I cried. I had never been unpopular before, and I could not understand it.

The next morning somebody said to me, 'Have you heard the news?'

'What news?' I replied.

'About Jenkins and Strode.'

'What's the news?' I asked.

'They climbed onto the roof last night. Jenkins fell, and Strode tried to save him. He couldn't, and they both fell to the ground. They're in the hospital now.'

He looked at me strangely and then continued: 'I think they're both very ill. Jenkins's parents have just arrived and Strode's parents are coming this afternoon.'

I said nothing, and the boy went away. I felt faint, happy and afraid at the same time. I was happy that Jenkins and Strode would not be able to attack me again. But I was afraid that they might die. Then everyone would say that their deaths were my fault. The school bell rang, and I walked towards the door. Two of the boys from my room came and shook hands with me. There was admiration on their faces. I whispered my thanks to the Virgin and the Lion.

My magic became famous immediately. Everyone wanted to know if I was going to use the third spell. Many boys now thought that Jenkins and Strode deserved to die. But I decided to let them live, and my kindness was noticed. I wrote several new spells to make my enemies better again. I did not write them in my diary because they might fail. The school waited silently for several days, while everyone hoped for the worst kind of news. But the health of Jenkins and Strode improved a little, and they were taken home. I took pleasure in the success of my spells.

'Are you vanquished, Colston, are you vanquished?' No, I was not. I had won by myself, without any human help. After that, the boys at school always came to me when they wanted advice about magic or spells. I used to demand threepence for any help that I gave them. I also became famous for my command of language. 'Vanquished' was my first long word, and it was followed by many others. It was then that I began to have hopes for the future: I decided to become a writer. Perhaps I would be the greatest writer of the greatest century, the twentieth.

In February, March and April 1900 I had written many notes in my diary, and most of these described my successes. There was not much in April because I was at home on holiday then. But May and the first half of June were full again, and then I reached the pages for July. On Monday 9th July I had written 'Brandham Hall'. There was a list of the other guests at the Hall. Then: 'Tuesday 10th 85 degrees'. Each day after that I had written the highest temperature and many other notes. At last I came to 'Thursday 26th 81 degrees'.

They were the last details I had written. I did not have to turn the other pages. I knew very well that they were all empty.

The main events of my life happened between 9th and 26th July 1900. They are my secret. They explain the kind of life that I have lived. For the past fifty years I have hidden them from the world, but I have never forgotten them.

I know a lot more today than I knew in 1900. If Brandham Hall had been the same kind of place as Southdown Hill School, I would have solved the problems in my own way. I understood the other pupils because they were a part of my life. But I did not understand Brandham Hall. The people there and their lives were different from those I knew. The other guests and our hosts seemed to have all the mystery of the stars.

There, in my mother's dusty room, I imagined a conversation between two people. One of them was Colston when he was a boy, thirteen years old. The other was myself, Colston, at the age of sixty-four.

'Why have you become a sad old man?' the boy asked. 'Your life is very uninteresting, isn't it? You've thrown your life away in lifeless offices and libraries. You've studied other people's books, but you haven't written any books yourself. What has happened to the Virgin and the Lion?'

I answered immediately: 'It was your fault. You were like an insect that flies round a bright flame. You flew close to the flame, and you were burned. That's why I am a dry, lifeless being.'

The boy replied, 'But that was fifty years ago! Are you still suffering? Don't you remember all your hopes for the twentieth century?'

I said, 'Has the twentieth century enjoyed more success than I have? Is everything as great as you expected? I don't think so. You were vanquished, Colston, and your great century has been vanquished, too.'

'But perhaps you didn't try hard enough,' he answered. 'You didn't need to accept defeat so easily. I didn't run away from Jenkins and Strode, did I? They were my enemies, and I had to destroy them. Have you done anything like that? Have you written any spells?'

'That was your business,' I answered, 'and when it mattered you didn't do it.'

'Oh, I did. I wrote a spell.'

'It was not strong enough. You didn't put a spell on Mrs Maudsley or her daughter or Ted Burgess or Trimingham. You refused to think of them as your enemies. You thought they were as wonderful as the beings of the stars. If you had put a terrible spell on them, I would have become a better man.'

'Try now,' he said, 'try now. It isn't too late.'

The conversation ended, but it had had an effect on me. I was thinking about Brandham Hall. It may not be too late, I thought. I will try to write the story. I began to feel excited.

It was very late. I picked up the lock again and turned it round in my hand. What was the secret of the letters that opened it? It was not a difficult question. I had not heard the word for many years, and I said it out loud. It was my own name, LEO.

Chapter 2 An Invitation

When I was at school, boys tried to forget their first names. I was Colston, not Leo Colston, and Maudsley was just called Maudsley. Later, perhaps, I shall remember his first name.

Maudsley and I were not special friends. With three other boys, he and I slept in the same room, and we knew one another well. He was pale, with fair hair and a round face. He was a year younger than I was. We often talked to each other and compared the personal things we owned. He told me that he lived at Brandham Hall, in Norfolk. I told him that my home was Court Place at West Hatch, near Salisbury.

Maudsley seemed to admire the name Court Place. He probably imagined that it was a large house in the country. His mother probably thought so, too, but they were both wrong. Court Place was quite an ordinary house in the main street of West Hatch.

Although it was not a big house, the costs were high. At that time my mother did not have a lot of money. My father had died when I was eleven. He had been the manager of a bank in Salisbury, and he had had many strange ideas. He refused to let me go to school, and taught me himself at home. We had very few friends. My mother and I had other ideas, though, and soon after his death I started at Southdown Hill School.

I admired my father and his opinions, but I always felt closer to my mother. My father was not interested in success, and this used to annoy my mother. She was very different from my father. She liked meeting people and talking to them. She was fond of fashionable clothes and social occasions, but my father preferred to stay at home with his books. He sometimes took her to parties, and she enjoyed these very much.

Maudsley and I never spoke to each other about our families. In some ways he seemed much older than the rest of us and was never in trouble with the other boys. He did not need the admiration for which I had to fight. He was always in agreement with public opinion, always on the winning side. I taught him how to write magic spells and did not make him pay for my advice. He admired me and my skills, and I enjoyed his admiration.

I enjoyed, too, the weeks that followed the defeat of Jenkins and Strode. I was well known for magic and had a safe position with the other pupils. In April I went home for the holidays.

My mother did not really understand my success. She was confused about my magic. I could not, of course, describe it to her in detail. I told her that a few of the boys had been unkind to me. Then I had written magic words in my diary. After that, the unkind boys had hurt themselves and I felt good about it.

She refused to share my success, saying sadly: 'You're too young to have enemies, Leo. You must be kind to them when they come back to school. I'm sure they didn't intend to be unkind to you.'

Jenkins and Strode did not return to school until the autumn. When I met them again, they were very quiet. I was quiet, too, and we were certainly kind to one another.

When I went back to school early in May, many boys asked

me to write more spells. I agreed to write a spell that would result in a holiday for the school. I put all my magic power into this spell, and I was soon successful. Two weeks later a fever hit the school. By the middle of June half the boys were sick. The headmaster told us that we would all have to go home. This was a great success for me.

Both Maudsley and I escaped the illness. Our heavy cases were brought into our room, and we filled them with our clothes and other things. All that day we smelt the beautiful smell of home. Next morning, two vehicles arrived at the door of the school. We said goodbye to the headmaster and his family, and then we drove off to the station.

When we took our seats in the train, there was happiness on every face.

I took my diary out of my pocket and found the date. It was Friday 15th June. With a red pencil I drew a line under the date while the other boys watched me. They probably thought I was thinking about some new spell. But I just filled the space with red lines. I believed that I was partly responsible for the illness at school; and the other boys thought so, too. I felt very confident of my power. If I *wanted* something to happen, it surely would happen.

At home, my mother spoke to me about the fever at school.

'You'll probably be ill, too, Leo,' she said. 'You must tell me as soon as you don't feel well.'

I smiled. 'I won't get that fever, Mother,' I said. 'I'm sure I won't.' I did not say that I would not get the fever because I did not want to get it.

'I hope you won't,' she said, 'but don't forget that you were very ill last year.'

I would never forget the year 1899 and its great unhappiness for me. In January my father had died after a short illness. In the summer I was seriously ill myself and had to stay in bed for seven weeks. July and August had been unusually hot months, too, but my own fever was even hotter. I was very happy when the summer ended.

I decided that the summer of 1900 would not be hot. On 1st July I was pleased that the temperature reached only sixty-four degrees. There had been three hot days, 10th, 11th and 12th June; and I had marked them in my diary with a cross.

The letter from Mrs Maudsley came on 1st July, and my mother showed it to me. Mrs Maudsley was also a little worried by the thought of illness.

'If our boys are well on 10th July,' she wrote, 'they will probably escape the fever. And I would be very pleased if you would allow Leo to stay with us for a few weeks. Marcus often talks about him, and I would like to meet him. Marcus is my youngest child and will be happy to have a friend for the holidays. His brother and sister are several years older and have their own friends. If you agree, we promise to take great care of Leo. The air here is dry and very good for children. My husband and I were not very well last winter, and we intend to stay here for the whole summer. I hope Leo will be able to stay with us until the end of July.'

Marcus. Yes, that was his first name. I remember it now.

I read the letter many times and could soon repeat it from memory. Someone who did not know me wanted to meet me. I believed that Mrs Maudsley was very interested in my character and activities. I did not guess that she would have written the same thing to any boy's mother.

At first my mother did not want me to go. She made all kinds of excuses.

'Norfolk is a long way, Leo,' she said, 'and you've never stayed with another family before.'

'I've had to stay at school,' I argued.

'Yes, but you'll be away for two or three weeks, and you may not like it.'

'I'm sure I shall enjoy it, Mother,' I said.

'And you'll be there on your birthday. Have you forgotten that? We've always been together on your birthday.'

It was true that I *had* forgotten my birthday. It was not a very happy thought, and I did not answer.

'Will you promise to write to me if you're not happy?' she said.

I knew I would be happy. But I did not want to say that to my mother. I promised to write, but she was still not satisfied.

'You may get that fever,' she said brightly, 'or perhaps Marcus will. You won't be able to go then.'

I asked her many times if she had written to Mrs Maudsley. Two or three days passed.

At last she said, 'Don't worry me, Leo. I have written, and you can go.'

I had to get ready. I had to decide about the things that I would need.

'I won't need summer clothes,' I said. 'I know it won't be hot.'

And I was right. The first days of July were not hot, and my mother agreed with me. She believed that thick clothes were safer than thin clothes. But also she could not afford to buy new clothes for me. If I had wanted thin clothes for the summer, she would have bought them. But I was certain that the weather would not be hot. And I did not want her to throw money away.

On 6th July I began to feel afraid myself and did not want to go to Norfolk. But my mother now refused to change the plan.

'Write to Mrs Maudsley, please,' I asked, 'and tell her that I'm ill.'

'I can't do that, Leo,' she said. 'It isn't true. You've been at home for three weeks. Mrs Maudsley would know that you weren't ill.'

I went to my room and wrote a spell. I wanted red spots on my body. But after two days no spots had appeared. On the last evening my mother and I sat together in silence. I think she wanted to give me some advice. But there were tears in my eyes, and she said nothing.

Chapter 3 Brandham Hall

I do not remember Brandham Hall very well. In my mind there are faint pictures of parts of the house, but the general view is not clear. My diary gives some of the facts.

I arrived on 9th July. That evening I wrote: 'Maudsley met me at the station and we drove thirteen and three-quarter miles to Brandham Hall.'

I cannot remember that drive at all. I have even forgotten the look of the house when I first saw it through the trees. But I had studied a book about the area, and had copied some of the details into my diary.

Brandham Hall is the home of the Winlove family. It is a big, rather ugly house on high ground, with gardens, a large park and a farm. The double stairs to the first floor are an interesting example of the builder's art. At present the house, gardens and park are rented by Mr W. H. Maudsley, of the City Bank, London.

I thought the double stairs were the most beautiful part of the house. The curve in them was more than half a complete circle. I compared them to many things: a new moon, a horseshoe. When I walked up or down those stairs, I used a different side each time.

Marcus and I slept together at the back of the house. There were stairs there, too, and they were convenient for our room.

'Are you going to put a spell on us here?'

The room had a wide window high in the wall. It was so high that we could see only the sky. Fifty years ago people did not worry about whether their children's rooms were pleasant or not, and ours was not very nice.

Many people came and went while I was staying at Brandham Hall. One evening, I remember, there were eighteen people at the table for dinner. I have never forgotten the brightness of the silver dishes and the small pink lights. The large figure of Mrs Maudsley seemed to command the table from one end, and the thin, straight figure of her husband was always at the other end.

Mr Maudsley was a slight little man and did not seem to run the house. I used to meet him suddenly on the stairs, and he usually stopped. When this happened, our conversation was always the same. He said, 'Are you enjoying the holiday?' I answered, 'Yes, sir.' Then he always said, 'That's good.' He was often in a hurry, but I do not know where he was going.

His wife clearly ran Brandham Hall, and in my memory she seems to have many faces. For fifty years she has been appearing regularly to me in my dreams. I have failed to keep her out of them. I actually saw her last on 26th July 1900. Her face then was so terrible that it was not really a face at all. It was a big, round, pale shape, with eyes that were dark and fixed. Wet, black hair fell over the eyes. When I dream about Mrs Maudsley, I never see that terrible look. In my dreams she is as kind to me as she was at the beginning of my visit. At that time I did not recognize the danger behind her influence.

My first meal at Brandham was dinner on 9th July. I was a new guest and sat next to Mrs Maudsley.

She smiled at me and said, 'Marcus has told me that you know a lot about magic. Is it true?'

I smiled, 'Oh, not really. But at school, everything is different.'

'Are you going to put a spell on us here?' she asked.

'Oh, no.' I remember that I felt surprised and confused. I had never expected that Marcus would tell his mother about the spells. They were a secret.

Mrs Maudsley never looked at anyone by chance but always for a purpose. Her look usually meant that she did not agree, or that she was annoyed. She seemed to look most often at her daughter, Marian, but Marian did not seem to notice the looks.

Marcus had introduced me to everyone and told me something about each one. I wrote their names in my diary. The young people were generally single and only a few years older than I was, but those few years seemed wider than an ocean. They were never very important to me or to Marcus. But Marian was important.

Denys, Mr and Mrs Maudsley's older son, was a tall young man with yellow hair. He had a high opinion of himself and also many other great opinions and plans. His mother was not very patient either with Denys or with his ideas. They did not seem to get on very well, although he tried to be the man of the family. This was really his father's position, but Mr Maudsley was quiet and did not seem to mind. It soon became clear to me that Mr Maudsley was a very rich man.

I did not notice any disagreements between Mr and Mrs Maudsley. She made plans for the family and for the guests, but he made plans only for himself. The rest of us usually accepted her decisions without argument. If anyone had doubts, he would receive one of her looks. That ended the discussion.

One day Marcus said to me, 'My sister is very beautiful.' This was a new fact that I had to learn. It seemed that he had just introduced me to her again. And when I saw her next, I looked at her closely.

Marian was very tall, and her eyes were very blue. Her face was round, like her mother's, but the colour was pink instead of almost white. When I saw her, she looked anxious. She was thinking about something, and her face had the look of some powerful bird. A moment later she looked up at me, and a great blue light shone from her eyes.

After that I knew how to recognize beauty, and I could always recognize Marian when she was with the other people at Brandham Hall.

My diary tells me about something which I had quite forgotten.

'Wednesday 11th July. I saw the deadly nightshade – *Atropa belladonna*.'

Marcus was not with me, and I was looking round some old huts behind the house. I had entered one which had no roof and suddenly saw the plant. It had already grown well and was about five feet tall. It was bright and strong and full of juice. I could almost see the juice that was rising in it.

Atropa belladonna, the deadly nightshade. I knew that every part of the plant was extremely poisonous. I noticed, too, that it was beautiful. I looked at its bright fruit and dark purple flowers. The flowers seemed to stretch out towards me. They would poison me, I thought then, even if I did not touch them. I wondered if I should tell Mrs Maudsley about my discovery. If I told her, she might have the plant destroyed. I did not want anyone to destroy all that beauty. In any case, I wanted to look at it again, and so I did not tell her.

Chapter 4 Marian's Promise

At first I was in trouble with the weather.

It had been cool on Monday when I travelled. The next day it was hot, and the sky was cloudless. Marcus and I escaped from the house after lunch.

Marcus said, 'Let's go and see the thermometer. It's one that marks the highest and the lowest temperatures of the day.'

I remember where the thermometer was. It hung on the wall of a mysterious building. The place stood in the shadow of an old tree and often attracted me.

'This marker shows the highest temperature,' Marcus explained, 'and that one shows the lowest.'

I wanted to move the markers, and Marcus must have guessed my thoughts.

'We mustn't touch it,' he said. 'It would make my father angry. He likes to take care of the thermometer himself.'

'Is he often angry?' I asked. I could not imagine him being angry.

Marcus replied, strangely, 'No, but my mother would be.'

The temperature was nearly eighty-three degrees. The marker would probably move up to eighty-five by teatime.

I was very warm, and I remembered my mother's frequent words. 'Try not to get hot,' she had said. How could I not get hot? I looked at Marcus. He was wearing a light suit, but it was eighty-three degrees and Marcus looked hot too.

I remember the details of our clothes. Marcus and I had our photograph taken, and the picture is in front of me now. I am wearing a heavy, white collar. My thick suit fits me tightly, from my neck to below my knees. I have thick, black socks on and a pair of heavy boots.

I still believed, partly at least, that I could influence the weather. That night I made up a strong spell. I hoped that it would reduce the temperature. But I was disappointed. After lunch on Wednesday it was eighty-five degrees. With an effort, I said to Marcus, 'Should I put on my games clothes?'

'No,' he replied quickly. 'It's not polite. No one should wear school clothes during the holidays. There's another thing that you mustn't do, Leo. When you take your clothes off at night, you put them carefully on a chair. You mustn't do that. You must leave them where they fall. The servants will pick them up.'

I believed every word that he said. I thought he was the height of fashion and good taste. In the same way he admired my skill in magic.

At teatime someone said to me, 'You look hot. Haven't you any lighter clothes?'

The words were spoken partly in fun. I ran my hand across my face and said, 'I'm not really hot. Marcus and I have been running.'

'Running?' said another voice. 'In this heat?' he laughed. And I shook a little. I imagined that I was at school again, and someone had shouted the word 'vanquished' at me.

Trouble started, although it was hidden by smiles and kind faces. From time to time they said, 'Hello, Leo. Are you still feeling hot? Why don't you take your coat off? You would be more comfortable without it.'

I hated these jokes. In those days, fifty years ago, everyone was particular about clothes. I took my coat off only when I went to bed. I knew that everyone was laughing at me, and I hated it.

That night I made a new spell. I felt so unhappy that I could not sleep. My diary was under the covers. I took it and managed to write the spell in the darkness. 'It will be stronger,' I thought, 'because it's in writing.'

I remember that the spell succeeded. The next day the temperature did not reach seventy-seven, and I felt calmer and cooler.

I did not look cool, and at teatime the jokes began again. Soon I felt very unhappy. I did not guess the intentions of the other people. They were trying to show kindness in order to make me talk.

I looked at myself in a mirror. For the first time I noticed my clothes and compared them with the others' clothes. I looked strange and unfashionable. I felt poor and common, and my face was red.

'I may look hot,' I said, 'but I'm cool inside.'

I thought it was a clever little speech, but everyone laughed loudly and tears came to my eyes. I drank some tea quickly.

Suddenly I heard Mrs Maudsley's voice. It was like a breath of cold air and it was blowing towards me.

'Did you leave your summer clothes at home?'

'No . . . yes . . . Mother forgot to pack them,' I said.

This was a lie, and also an unkindness to my mother. She would have bought me lighter clothes if I had wanted them. I began to cry.

Mrs Maudsley said calmly, 'Why don't you write to her? Ask her to send them.'

I did not answer, but Marian spoke. I do not think she had ever said anything about the heat to me.

She now said, 'The post is too slow, Mother. I'll take him to Norwich tomorrow and buy some new clothes for him.' She said to me, 'You'd like that, wouldn't you?'

'Yes,' I whispered, 'but . . .'

'But what?'

'I haven't enough money.'

'We've got some,' Marian said.

'Oh, I can't take yours,' I said. 'Mother won't like that.'

Marian said, 'The new things can be a birthday present. His mother wouldn't mind that, I'm sure. When is your birthday, Leo?'

'It's . . . actually, it's on the twenty-seventh.'

'Of this month?'

'Yes. I was born under the sign of Leo. But Leo isn't my real name.'

'What is your real name?'

'It's Lionel. You won't tell anyone, will you?'

'Why not?'

'Because it's unusual.'

She tried to understand this mystery of a boy's mind. Then she said, 'That's good. You'll be here on your birthday. You can have something from each of us. Clothes are the nicest presents, aren't they? If you were born under the sign of Leo, you should wear a lion skin.'

'That might be too hot,' I said in fun.

'Yes, of course,' she said. 'We'll go to Norwich tomorrow.'

'Perhaps you should wait until Monday,' her mother said. 'Hugh will be here then, and you can go together.'

'Who will be here?' Marian asked.

'Hugh. He's coming on Saturday. Didn't you know?'

'Are you sure, Mother?' Denys asked. 'He told me that he was going to watch the horses at Goodwood.'

'I had a letter from him yesterday,' Mrs Maudsley said.

'I don't want to argue, Mother,' Denys said. 'But Trimingham won't miss Goodwood.'

I wondered who Hugh or Trimingham was. It would be annoying if he got in the way of Marian's plans. I felt angry and jealous. If Trimingham came with us, the trip would not be as exciting.

'Don't you agree, Marian?' Mrs Maudsley repeated. 'It will be better if you go on Monday.'

Marian had decided to go the next day.

'Hugh won't enjoy it, Mother,' she said. 'He knows Norwich better than we do. And if we wait until Monday, Leo will be half dead from the heat. Does anyone want to come with us?'

She looked at everyone in the room. Her question was not really an invitation, and no one wanted to come. I could not hide my happiness.

'May we go, Mother?' Marian asked.

'Of course – but does your father want the horses?'

Mr Maudsley shook his head.

'Go to Challow and Crawshay's,' said Denys suddenly. 'It's the best shop. Trimingham buys his ties there.'

'Does Leo need ties?' Mrs Maudsley asked.

'I'll pay for a tie if you promise to buy it at Challow's,' Denys said. I began to feel hot again.

Marian decided to find out what things I needed. She had to examine my clothes. I hated the thought of this, but I need not have worried. When she came into our room with Marcus, she was very kind. She looked at my things carefully.

'They have been mended beautifully,' she said.

I did not tell her that my mother had done the work; but perhaps she guessed. She was good at guessing.

'You haven't any summer clothes at home, have you?' she said. I agreed, and felt happy. I was happy to share the secret with her. But I wondered how she knew.

Chapter 5 A Trip to the River

After the trip to Norwich everything was different. Marian and I went to several shops and looked at a lot of clothes. I put on some of the things, and Marian liked them.

'That looks nice, Leo,' she said. 'It's just right for you.'

There were other things that she did not like. We did not buy them because they did not look nice. In Marian's opinion it was most important that clothes should look good.

We had lunch at a hotel, and it was a great event for me. My father had always said that meals in hotels were too expensive. After lunch we bought a few more things.

'Would you like to change your clothes now?' Marian asked.

It was a question that I had to think about. It was hot, and I was wearing my thick suit. But I decided to put off the pleasure of changing mainly because I was too excited to feel the heat. Everything seemed to depend on Marian being there. She made me think of a bright, colourful bird.

When we had bought all the things, she said: 'Leo, would you like to amuse yourself for an hour? I have something to do. You can visit the church.'

I agreed immediately. And when she left, the good feeling stayed with me. I knew of course that I would soon see her again. Inside the church I looked up at the great curves of the roof. The building seemed to express all my thoughts; it was high and wide and strong. Later, when I stood outside, I looked up again. I tried to see where the high roof seemed to meet the sky. All my thoughts were as high as that great roof.

Marian and I had agreed to meet at four o'clock. I looked around for Marian and saw her down the street. I noticed that a man near her touched his hat. It seems clear to me now that she was saying goodbye to him. She walked slowly towards me.

That day in Norwich my character seemed to change. I began to feel like the other people at Brandham Hall. When I saw them all in the evening, I was wearing my new clothes. Everyone thought I looked wonderful. I was told to stand on a chair and to turn round.

'Doesn't he look cool?' someone said.

'As cool as the grass outside,' said another, 'and the same colour too.'

They discussed the colour of my new green suit.

'Don't you *feel* different?' somebody asked me.

'Yes,' I replied happily, 'I feel like another person.'

They laughed, and then the conversation changed. They began to talk about something other than my new suit. I had enjoyed being the centre of attention. I got down from the chair.

Mrs Maudsley called me and I went to her anxiously. I felt like some insect that was caught in a bright light. She held the soft material of my suit between her fingers.

'I think it's very nice,' she said. 'I hope your mother will think

I noticed that a man near her touched his hat.

so, too.' Then she turned away from me and spoke to her daughter.

'Oh, Marian, did you have time to buy those things I asked you to?'

'Yes, Mother, I bought them.'

'And did you buy anything for yourself?'

'Oh, no, Mother. I'll buy them later. There's lots of time.'

'You mustn't wait too long,' said Mrs Maudsley, calmly. 'Did you meet anyone in Norwich?'

'Nobody at all. We were busy all the time, weren't we, Leo?'

'Yes, we were,' I answered. I wanted to agree with her so much that I forgot my visit to the church.

I now began to enjoy the hot weather. I liked to feel the heat on my skin. The green suit was made of thin cloth, and it had an open neck. My trousers were short and my new socks were thin and cool. But I was especially proud of my new shoes, partly because they were just like Marcus's. All these things helped me to enjoy the heat of summer.

New clothes always seem to make a person feel better. I certainly could not hide the pleasure that mine gave me. But I felt grateful, too, and very surprised. I was grateful for the kindness of my hosts because they had bought all these things. And I was surprised that the cost had seemed quite unimportant. In one morning Marian had probably spent on my clothes more than my mother spent in a year. Marcus's family must be richer than I had ever imagined. And there were other things that I could not understand. I did not know that rich people, like Mr Maudsley, did not need to go to work. I wondered why everyone seemed to be on holiday all the time. I tried to guess something about the families of the young men and women who came to stay at Brandham Hall. This last problem particularly interested me, and I explained it in my own way: I compared them with the beings in the star signs.

I now had a swimsuit and wanted to wear it. I could only swim if somebody was holding me. Marian said that one of them would do that, but Mrs Maudsley refused to allow it.

'If you want to swim, Leo,' she said, 'you must get your mother's permission. In her letter she said that you were a little weak. When the others swim this afternoon, you had better watch them.'

I wrote to my mother immediately and then hurried away with the others. It was Saturday 14th July and the weather was a disappointment to me. The temperature was only seventy-six degrees. I took my swimsuit with me in order to feel that I was one of the group.

We walked together down the path. There were Marian and Denys, another young man and a young woman, and Marcus and I. It was about six o'clock and still warm. We passed through a little gate and entered a group of trees. Under the trees it was dark and cool, almost cold. Later during the holiday, I often went that way through the trees, but I never again felt the same shock of coldness. We ran down a steep bank into a field, and it was hot again.

Marcus said, 'Trimingham is coming this evening.'

'Oh, is he?' I answered. 'Is he nice?'

'Yes, but very ugly. You mustn't look surprised by his face or it will annoy him. He doesn't like people feeling sorry for him. He was hurt in the war. The doctors say his face will never improve.'

'Bad luck,' I said.

'Yes, but you mustn't say so to him or to Marian.'

'Why not?'

'Mother won't like it.'

'Why not?' I said again.

'If I tell you, will you promise not to tell anyone?'

I promised.

'Mother wants Marian to marry him.'

I thought about this news in silence. I did not like it at all. I already felt jealous of Trimingham, and this news about what had happened to him in the war made it worse. Other people would have a high opinion of him because he had fought for his country. My father had hated war, and I agreed with him. Perhaps Trimingham deserved to be ugly.

We came to the end of the field. A short distance in front there was a tall, black platform. It had wooden posts and bars, and it frightened me a little. I wondered why we were walking towards it. Suddenly we saw a man's head and shoulders near the platform. He climbed up onto the platform. For a moment he stood still, and then he jumped off the top. I knew then that the river was near.

'This place is private,' Denys said. 'That man shouldn't be here. What shall we do? Shall I order him to leave?'

'We'll have to let him dress first,' the other man said.

'He can dress in five minutes, and then he'll have to go,' Denys said.

'I'm going to change my clothes,' Marian said. 'I need more than five minutes for that.'

She went away with the young woman. There was a hut on the bank of the river, and the women changed there.

The water suddenly appeared, and we walked down to it. There was a pool that looked as blue as the sky. The only thing on its surface was the man's head. He saw us and began to swim towards us. We could soon see his face.

'Ah, that's Ted Burgess,' Denys said. 'He lives at Black Farm. We shouldn't be rude to him. He rents the land on the other side of the river. Trimingham wouldn't like it if we were rude to him. I'll just say how do you do to him. He isn't one of our friends, of course; but he mustn't think that we're too proud to talk to him.'

Burgess climbed out of the water with difficulty, Denys helping him.

'Why didn't you get out comfortably?' Denys said. 'We've had some steps made on the other side of the platform.'

'I know,' the man replied. 'But I've always got out here.'

I remember his voice now. He spoke in the local way, and I thought he wanted to tell Denys he was sorry.

'I didn't know that you would be here,' he said. 'I've been working in the fields, and I was very hot. I won't stay long.'

'Oh, you needn't hurry,' Denys said. 'We were hot, too, at the Hall. Oh, did you know that Trimingham will be here tonight? He'll probably want to see you.'

'Perhaps he will,' Burgess said. Then he climbed up to the platform again and jumped into the water.

Denys said, 'I don't think I made him feel uncomfortable.'

His friend agreed, and they went towards some small trees on the bank. Marcus and I went another way and soon found a place to change our clothes. We were completely hidden by the tall grass that grew beside the river.

Marcus said, 'You needn't put on your swimsuit if you're not going to swim. It would look strange.'

He always seemed to know what was best, so I did not take my clothes off.

A few minutes later we all arrived at the steps beside the platform. Denys and his friend pulled each other into the deep water. Marian, the other girl and Marcus stayed in the water by the steps. At first they played, throwing up the water with their hands; and they were all laughing. Then the young women began to swim across the pool.

I did not like watching them, so I walked round to the other side of the platform. Denys and his friend were lying on their backs in the water. While I was admiring them, Ted Burgess climbed out of the water.

I moved back into the tall grass where he could not see me and I watched him. His body looked so powerful that it almost frightened me. He walked away from the bank and lay down on the warm ground in the sun. What did it feel like, I wondered, to be as strong as he was? He did not need to play games or to do exercises. His body was complete and perfect and existed for its own strength and beauty.

Suddenly a cry came from the river: 'Oh, my hair! My hair! It's all wet! It'll never dry now. I'm coming out!'

Ted Burgess jumped up. He did not dry himself. He pulled his shirt and trousers on, over his wet swimsuit, and put on his socks and boots. In half a minute he was dressed. Then he walked quickly away.

A moment later Marian came out of the water. She was holding her long hair in front of her, like the Virgin of the stars. She saw me immediately and seemed happy and angry at the same time.

'Oh, Leo,' she said, 'you look so pleased with yourself that I'd like to throw you in the river!'

Her words frightened me, and perhaps my fear showed. She then said, 'I don't mean that really. But you're very *dry* and I'm very *wet*.' She looked round and added, 'Has that man gone?'

'Yes,' I said. I was always glad to answer any question she asked me. 'He went in a hurry. His name is Ted Burgess, and he lives at Black Farm. Do you know him?'

'I may have met him,' Marian said. 'I don't remember. But I'm happy that you're still here.'

I did not quite know why she was happy, but it sounded as if she was saying something nice about me. She went to the hut. Soon the others came out of the river. We had to wait a long time for the ladies. But at last Marian came out of the hut, still holding her hair in front of her.

'Oh, I shall never get it dry,' she cried. 'And the water is running over my dress.'

I was surprised to hear Marian talk like that. Her hair was wet, and she was behaving like a child. Suddenly I had an idea.

'Here's my swimsuit,' I said. 'It's *quite* dry. You can put it round your neck so that it hangs down your back. Then you can spread your hair on it, and your hair will soon dry. Your dress won't get wet either.'

'It might be a good idea,' she said.

The other girl hung the swimsuit round Marian's neck, and everyone smiled at my cleverness.

'And now you must spread my hair on it,' she said to me. 'And please don't pull it. Oh, Leo!'

I knew that I had not hurt her. I had not really touched her hair. Then I saw that she was smiling. I started again, spreading it gently over my swimsuit. It was a duty that I loved; partly, perhaps, because I loved Marian.

I walked back with her through the shadows. Once or twice she asked me how her hair was. In order to answer her I had to feel it. She then joked that I had pulled it. She was strangely excited, and I was, too. In some way I thought that we were both excited for the same reason. But I could not have explained this idea. I believed that I had done a wonderful service to Marian. At the Hall she took off the swimsuit and gave it back to me. It was wet with the wetness from which I had saved her. She let me touch her hair. It was dry with the dryness that I had given her. I had never felt happier in my life.

Chapter 6 Marcus Falls Ill

It was Sunday 15th July; my first Sunday morning at Brandham Hall. Marcus did not come down to breakfast with me. He did not feel well and wanted to stay in bed. He looked hot and his eyes were bright.

'Don't worry about me,' he said. 'One of the servants will soon come up. Give my greetings to Trimingham.'

I decided to tell Mrs Maudsley about Marcus. I was anxious about his health and rather liked telling bad news. I waited until the bell rang at nine o'clock, and then went down the double stairs. I easily remembered the side that had to be used.

What was Trimingham like, I wondered. He was not called Mr Trimingham, but Mrs Maudsley still wanted her daughter to marry him. Perhaps Marian did not want to marry him. There would certainly be trouble if Marian's wishes were not satisfied. I felt quite sure of that.

I reached my favourite chair. The other guests were coming in, and one of them sat down beside me. I immediately knew who it was. Although Marcus had told me about him, I could not hide my shock.

His face looked terrible. Between one eye and the corner of his mouth there was a great curved line in his skin. It pulled the eye down and the mouth up. I did not think that he could shut that eye at all. His mouth, too, was probably always partly open. His whole face was the wrong shape. The side with the curved line was much shorter than the other.

I have tried to remember my exact thoughts when I first saw Trimingham. First I decided that I could not possibly like him. And when I had decided that, I immediately liked him better. I was certainly not afraid of him, but his social position was still not clear to me. It was not so high that it deserved the word 'Mr', but it was probably higher than Ted Burgess's position. Because of the damage to his face, I thought, everyone behaved very politely to him. But perhaps he was a poor relation of Mr or Mrs Maudsley, and they were kind to him for that reason. I decided, then, to be kind to him myself.

At breakfast he sat beside Marian, and so I could not give him the greetings from Marcus.

Several guests had arrived on Saturday night, and the table was full. Mrs Maudsley was very busy. During the meal she looked often and directly at Trimingham. She did not look at me until we were all leaving the table. Then she said: 'Oh, isn't Marcus here?' She had not noticed that he was absent.

She went to his room immediately. A few minutes later I followed her. Marcus was alone again.

'What's the matter?' I said.

'You'd better not stay here,' he replied. 'My head is aching, and I have some spots. It may be the same fever that the boys had in school.'

'That's bad luck,' I said. 'We left school weeks ago.'

'The doctor is coming. He'll know what it is. It will be fun if you get it, too. Perhaps we'll all get it. Then we won't be able to have the cricket match or the dance or anything. Oh, I shall laugh!'

'Are we going to have a cricket match?' I asked.

'Yes, we have one every year.'

'And a dance?' I asked. I was rather frightened of dancing.

'Yes. That's for Marian and Trimingham, and all the neighbours. It will be on Saturday the 28th. Mother has sent all the invitations, but the house will be like a hospital by then!'

We both laughed; Marcus said, 'You'd better go. You'll catch my fever.'

'Yes, I probably will.'

'Are you going to church?' he asked.

'Yes, I think so.'

I waved goodbye to him and ran down the double stairs. Several people were waiting at the front door. I was wearing my thick suit. Marcus had said that that was right. I could put on my green suit after lunch.

The church was only half a mile away, just past the cricket field. We walked in small groups. Marian walked with me and I told her about Marcus.

'Oh, he'll soon be well,' she said. 'The heat worries some people.'

'Is your hair quite dry now?' I asked, anxiously.

She laughed and said, 'Yes. I was glad to have your swimsuit.'

I felt proud of my idea, but conversation with her was not easy. I asked another question about her hair, and it made her laugh again.

'Haven't you any sisters?' she said.

That annoyed me, because I had told her about my family. Then she remembered one of our conversations in Norwich.

'Of course,' she said. 'I remember it perfectly now. I have many things to think about. I'm sorry that I forgot about your family.'

I had never heard Marian say sorry to anyone before. I had a strange feeling of sweetness and power, but I could not say anything to her. I looked at her face, at her large hat and at her light blue skirt. Suddenly I noticed that Trimingham was following us. He was walking quite quickly and would soon catch up with us. I did not want him to do that, but I did not know how to stop it.

'Trimingham is coming,' I said. It sounded like bad news.

'Oh, is he?' she said. She turned her head but did not call to him.

When he caught up with us, he smiled. He walked past us to the people in front, and I felt very glad.

Chapter 7 The Ninth Viscount

In church I sat with the family and their guests. Our seats were a little higher than the other seats. On one wall of the church there were metal plates with the names of dead people on them. I noticed that the name Trimingham appeared on each one. 'In memory of Hugh Winlove, Sixth Viscount Trimingham,' I read. 'Born 1783, died 1856.' I studied the names with care. Most of the Viscounts were called Hugh. There were seven of them, but there were two missing. There were no plates for the fifth Viscount or the ninth Viscount. The last name was Hugh, Eighth Viscount Trimingham, born 1843, died 1894.

I felt annoyed with the list because it was not complete. Where was the fifth Viscount? And the eighth Viscount had died in 1894, and so there must be another.

Suddenly the idea came to me that the ninth Viscount might still be alive. If that was true, it would change my opinion of the family. The names on the wall were a part of history. But if there was a ninth Viscount, he would probably be alive. He was not yet a part of history. He was a part of today, just as I was. The church, the village and Brandham Hall belonged to him. I wondered where he was.

Thinking about this, I decided to give part of my admiration to Mr Maudsley. He should enjoy it because he rented Brandham Hall. And if he enjoyed it, then I should enjoy it, too; because I was one of his guests.

I did not like being in church for a long time. The priest often talked about how bad men were. It was not true, I thought. I did not believe that people were really bad. In my opinion, people behaved in natural ways. Sometimes their acts caused pain or unhappiness. I thought of Jenkins and Strode. Were they bad boys? No. They were boys like myself. Life had its difficulties, and these tested any man. They proved he was brave, and being brave was a good thing.

When I was young, I greatly admired goodness. In my opinion, it was not the opposite of being bad. It was something strong and bright, like the sun, and did not change. All the Viscounts whose names I had read seemed to have goodness. The Maudsley family seemed to have it too, perhaps, I thought, because they paid rent for it. I believed that they were all different from ordinary people.

I looked at my watch. It was ten minutes to one. We stood up and went out of the church. Outside, I was alone again. Marian went ahead with some other people, but I was not last in the line. Trimingham was talking to the priest at the door. Everyone was very polite to Trimingham. I was thinking about this when he caught up with me.

He said very formally, 'We haven't been introduced yet. My name is Trimingham.'

At that time my experience of social customs was slight. I did not know that I should say my own name. Actually, I thought then that he was rather stupid. Did he imagine that I did not know his name?

'How do you do, Trimingham?' I replied.

'You may call me Hugh if you like,' he said.

'But your name is Trimingham, isn't it?' I said. 'You told me it was.' But I wanted to show him that I was polite, too. And I added quickly: 'Mr Trimingham, I mean.'

'You were right the first time,' he said.

I looked at his terrible face. I wondered if he was trying to make a joke.

'Aren't all men called "Mr"?' I asked.

'No, not all. Doctors aren't, are they?'

'But that's different. "Doctor" is a title.'

'I have a title, too,' he said.

And then, very slowly, I understood.

'Are you Viscount Trimingham?' I asked.

'Yes.'

'Are you the *ninth* Viscount Trimingham?'

'I am,' he said.

The news was a shock to me, and for a few moments I could not say anything. I felt annoyed then because no one had told

'My name is Trimingham.'

me, although it explained everyone's politeness to him.

'Shouldn't I call you "my lord"?' I asked.

'Oh, no,' he said, 'not in ordinary conversation. On some occasions perhaps you should, but Trimingham or Hugh is quite good enough.'

I was surprised now that he spoke in an ordinary way. I had to change my opinion of him very quickly. The old Trimingham started to disappear from my life. The ninth Viscount almost filled it. And I believed that he was nine times better than the first.

'You haven't told me your name,' he said.

'It's Colston,' I said, with some difficulty.

'Mr Colston?' he asked, gently.

'My first name is Leo.'

'Then I shall call you Leo if you agree.'

'Please do,' I said.

'Does Marian call you Leo?'

'Oh, yes, she does,' I replied excitedly. 'And I call her Marian, too. She told me to do that. Don't you think she's a wonderful girl?'

'Yes, I do,' he said.

'She's the nicest girl I've ever met,' I said. 'I'd do anything for her.'

'What would you do?'

I had a feeling that he was asking this question for a purpose.

I said, 'If a big dog attacked her, I would frighten it away. I could carry things for her, too, and be her messenger.'

'That would be a great help,' Lord Trimingham said, 'and it would be kind, too. Will you take a message to her now?'

'Of course. What shall I say?'

'Tell her that I've got her book. She left it in church.'

I hurried away. Marian was walking with a man I had not met. I did not interrupt their conversation, but a moment later they stopped talking.

I then said to Marian: 'Hugh asked me to give you a message. He said he had your book. You left it in church.'

'That was careless, wasn't it?' she said. 'I seem to forget everything. Please thank him for me.'

I ran back to Lord Trimingham and repeated Marian's words.

'Is that all she said?' he asked. He seemed disappointed. Perhaps he wanted her to come and claim the book immediately.

At the Hall a small vehicle with black and yellow wheels was standing outside the front door.

'Do you know whose that is?' Lord Trimingham asked.

'No.'

'It's Dr Franklin's. Doctors always come at lunchtime, don't they? It's one of their customs.'

'How did you know it was Dr Franklin's?' I asked.

'Oh, I know everyone in this part of Norfolk,' he said.

'Of course, it all belongs to you really, doesn't it?' I asked. Then I said something that I had been thinking about. 'You are a guest in your own house!'

He smiled. 'Yes, and I'm very pleased about it,' he said.

After lunch Mrs Maudsley said to me, 'Marcus isn't very well. The doctor said that he must stay in bed for a few days. We don't think it's a fever, but you'd better not see him until he's well again. The servants are moving your things into another room. It's a room with a green door. Shall I show it to you?'

'Oh, no, thank you,' I said. 'I know the room with a green door.'

I hurried away to see the room. It was small, with a very narrow bed, just big enough for one person. My things were all there. I checked them quickly: hair brushes, clothes, cases. They were all in different places, and they looked different. The room made me feel different, too. I imagined that I had a new character.

I remembered Marcus's suggestion. I put on my green suit and got ready to go out. There was a feeling of adventure in everything I did. I went silently down the stairs and out of the house.

Chapter 8 A Letter from Ted Burgess

The temperature was eighty-four degrees, and I wanted it to go higher.

There had been no rain at all, and I was enjoying the heat. It seemed to make my desires stronger. I was not now satisfied with a boy's simple experiences. I wanted larger experiences and more of them. Now I was close to the riches of the Maudsleys and the greatness of the Triminghams. These new experiences made me dream of power, and soon my dreams began to confuse me. I began to feel that I was a part of the star system. It was probably the heat that made me think in this way.

Marcus was in bed, and I had to amuse myself. In the afternoons we had usually played behind the house, but I now decided to go further. I walked along the path that led to the swimming place.

I was wondering if Ted Burgess, the farmer, would be there. But no one was swimming, and the silence of the place frightened me. I climbed the platform from which the farmer had jumped. I looked down into the clear water. It was like a mirror. I crossed a low bridge to the other side of the river and came to a field. There was a gate in the opposite corner of the field, and I walked towards that.

From the gate a path led between more fields to a low hill. It turned left then and ended at a small farmhouse. I opened the gate to the farm and went in. There, in front of me, was a haystack with a convenient ladder beside it.

I climbed the ladder to the top of the haystack and then threw myself down. The rush through the air gave me a good feeling. It was beautifully cool. I imagined that I was flying. But at the bottom my knee hit something hard. It was a large piece of wood that was buried in the hay on the ground. I watched the blood as it rushed out from a long cut just below my knee.

The farmer came out of the house. It was Ted Burgess.

'Who are you?' he cried. 'And what are you doing here?' He was very angry. 'I'll give you a good beating.'

His voice frightened me. I remembered how strong he was.

'But I know you!' I cried. 'We – we've met before!'

'Met?' he said. 'Where?'

'At the swimming place,' I said. 'You were swimming by yourself, and I came with the others.'

'Ah!' he said. His voice changed completely. 'You must be from the Hall.'

'Yes.' The pain in my knee was worse now, and I touched the cut.

'I'd better put something round that,' he said. 'Come to the house. Can you walk?'

He helped me to get up, and I went with him.

'You're lucky,' he said. 'It's Sunday today. If it was any other day, I wouldn't be here at this time. I heard you crying.'

'Did I cry?' The news was a shock to me.

'You did,' he said. 'But some boys cry a lot louder when they hurt themselves.' I enjoyed his kind words. I thought that perhaps I should say something nice to him, too.

'I saw you in the pool,' I said. 'You swim very well.'

He seemed pleased, and then said: 'I'm sorry I was angry. I have a quick temper. I didn't know that you were from the Hall.'

I thought that this change in the way he behaved to me was quite natural. It was right, too. Had I not changed my opinion of Lord Trimingham? He told me that he was a Viscount, and I changed my opinion of him immediately. Ted Burgess and I had

'Who are you?' he cried. 'And what are you doing here?'

the same ideas about correct behaviour towards other people.

We entered the house. I thought it was a very poor place.

'This is where I usually live,' he said. 'I'm not a rich farmer who pays men to work for him. I do most of the work myself. Sit down, and I'll get something for your knee.'

He washed the cut and then poured some special liquid on to it.

'You were lucky that you didn't tear your trousers or your socks,' he said. 'Or damage that nice green suit.'

I agreed with him. I had been very lucky. 'Miss Marian gave it to me,' I said. 'Miss Marian Maudsley, at the Hall.'

'Oh, did she?' he said. 'I don't know those people very well. I'll put this round the cut.'

'This' was a piece of cloth.

I stood up and walked about. My knee was beginning to feel better. I was already planning the story that I should tell at Brandham Hall. But I wanted to pay back the farmer's kindness. I looked round the empty kitchen and wondered if he needed anything.

Then I said: 'Thank you very much, Mr Burgess. You've helped me a lot. Is there anything that I can do for you?'

I quite expected that he would say 'No'. But I was wrong. He looked at me closely and said: 'Perhaps there is. Will you take a message for me?'

'Of course,' I said, but I felt disappointed. I remembered that Lord Trimingham's message to Marian had not been a great success. 'What is it, and who shall I give it to?'

He was still looking at me. Then he said, 'How old are you?'

'I shall be thirteen on the twenty-seventh of this month,' I replied.

'I thought you were older than that,' he said. 'I wonder if I can depend on you.'

His doubt gave me a shock, but I was not really annoyed.

'Of course you can,' I said proudly. 'My mother has just had a report from my school. It said that anyone could depend on me.'

'Yes, but can I be sure of you?' he said, slowly. 'My message will be a secret one.'

I thought he was very stupid. He clearly did not know that schoolboys do not tell secrets.

'Do you want me to promise that I'll tell no one?' I asked.

'You can do anything you like,' he answered. 'But if you tell anybody . . .' He did not finish the sentence, and I understood. It seemed to fill the room with a sense of power.

'There are a lot of people at the Hall, I expect,' he said. 'Are you ever alone with anybody?'

'Sometimes,' I said. 'I talked to Viscount Trimingham this morning. And once I went to Norwich with Marian. She's Marcus's sister and a wonderful girl.'

'Oh, you went to Norwich with her, did you?' the farmer said. 'Are you one of her special friends?'

'She's different from the others,' I said. 'She talks to me quite often. She talked to me this morning while we were going to church.'

'Oh, did she?' the farmer said. 'Are you alone with her sometimes?' He spoke with great seriousness. I thought that he was trying to imagine the scene.

I said, 'Sometimes we sit together, after dinner perhaps.'

'You sit together,' he repeated. 'Are you near enough to give her something?'

'Give her something? Oh, yes, I could do that!' I said.

'Could you give her a letter? A secret letter?'

It was such a simple request that I almost laughed. 'Oh, yes,' I said.

'I'll write it now,' he said. 'You'll wait, won't you?'

'Of course. But how can you write to her when you don't know her?'

'Who said I didn't know her?' he asked.

'You did. You said you didn't know the people at the Hall. And Marian told me that she didn't know you. She said that she may have met you; but she didn't remember you.'

The farmer thought for a moment. Then he said, 'She does know me. I don't visit the Hall, but we do some business together.'

'Is it a secret?' I asked, excitedly.

'It's more than a secret,' he said.

I suddenly felt weak, and Ted Burgess noticed this.

'Sit down,' he said. 'I'll soon write this letter.'

He brought a bottle of ink, a pen and a sheet of paper. But he was not used to writing. His fingers seemed too big to hold the pen.

At last he finished writing the letter. He put it in an envelope and stuck it down. I stretched out my hand, but he did not give me the letter.

'Give it to her when you are alone with her,' he said.

'You can be sure of that,' I said.

I thought, then, that he would really give it to me. But he held it tightly in his hand. He was like a lion guarding something.

'Can I depend on you?' he said.

'Of course you can,' I answered. His doubts annoyed me now.

'If any other person reads it, there will be a lot of trouble. There will be trouble for her and for me and perhaps for you, too.'

'I shall defend it until I die,' I said.

He smiled, opened his hand and pushed the letter towards me.

'Must she answer it?' I wanted to be sure about the details.

'She may answer it,' he said. 'But don't ask questions. Why do you want to know everything?'

I did not answer him but looked at my watch. 'It's late,' I said. 'I must go now.'

'How does your knee feel?' he asked.

'There's no pain. And it isn't bleeding now.'

'It may bleed when you walk,' he said.

I hoped it would bleed. I wanted to arrive at the Hall with blood on the cloth. I put the letter in the pocket of my trousers.

'May I come and play on your haystack again?' I asked.

'Of course. And I'll move that piece of wood.'

He walked with me to the gate, and we waved goodbye to each other.

◆

At Brandham Hall my knee became the subject of conversation. I explained that Ted Burgess had been very kind.

'Ah, he lives at Black Farm,' Mr Maudsley said. 'I've heard something about him. He's a strong young man and rides a horse well.'

'Yes. I want to see him,' Lord Trimingham said. 'He'll probably play in the cricket match on Saturday, and I'll talk to him then.'

Marian suddenly stood up and said, 'I'd better wash your knee, Leo. That cloth isn't very clean.'

I was glad to follow her up the stairs. She made me sit on the side of the bath and took off my shoe and sock. She washed the cut and put a clean cloth around it. Ted Burgess's cloth was lying on the side of the bath. It was covered with blood.

'Is that his?' she asked.

'Yes. He said he didn't want it. Shall I throw it away?'

'Perhaps I'll wash it,' she said. 'It's quite a nice piece of cloth.'

Then I remembered the letter and took it out of my pocket.

'He asked me to give you this,' I said.

She pulled it out of my hand. She had no pockets in her dress.

'These dresses are annoying,' she said. 'But wait a moment.'

Taking the letter and the cloth, she left the room. A moment later she came back and said: 'Now I must cover your knee.'

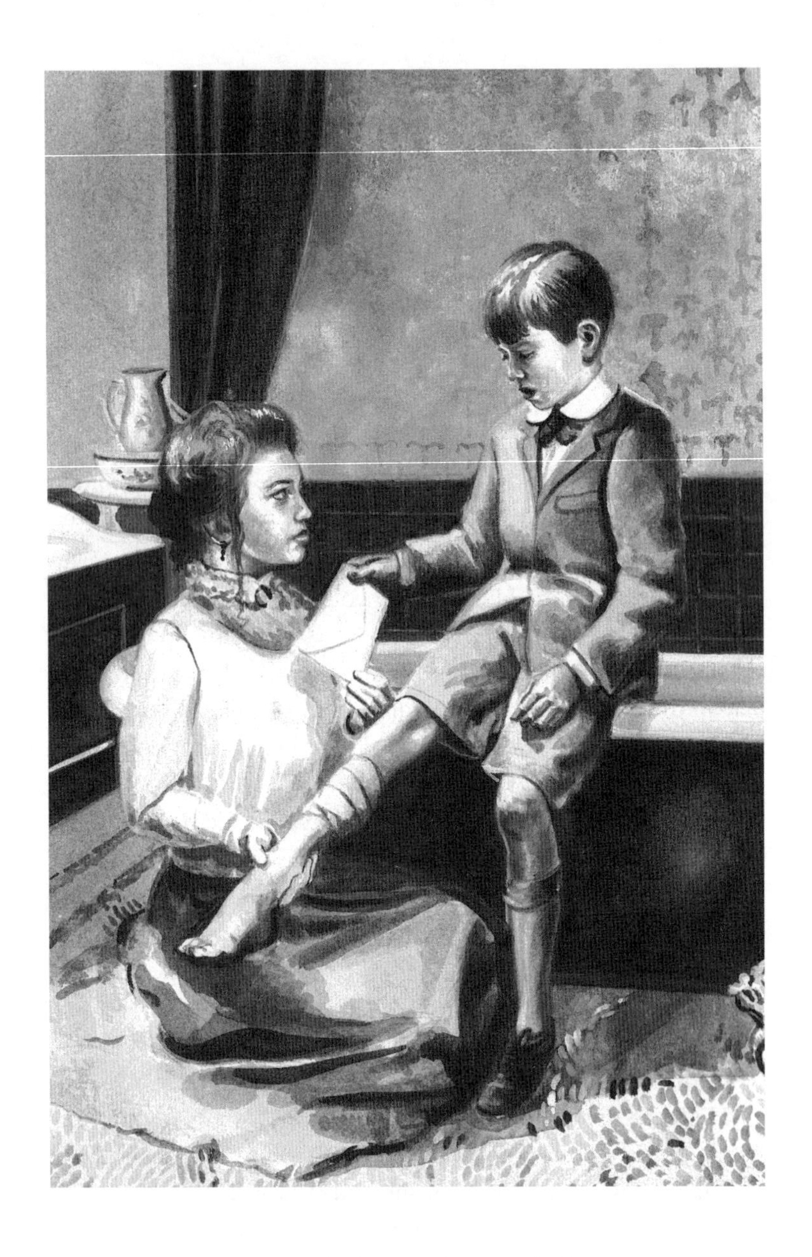

'He asked me to give you this.'

'But you've already done it!' I said.

'Of course I have! What am I thinking about? I must put on your sock.'

'Oh, I can do that myself,' I said. 'It's no trouble.'

But she wanted to do it, and I did not say anything.

'Are you going to answer the letter?' I asked.

She shook her head. 'You mustn't tell anyone about the letter.' She was looking away from me. 'Don't tell anyone, not even Marcus.'

Her fear and Ted Burgess's fear surprised me very much. They did not seem to know that it was a lot easier to keep silent than to speak.

'You needn't worry,' I said. 'I won't tell anyone. I can't tell Marcus, can I? I'm not allowed to see him.'

'Of course,' she said. 'I seem to forget everything. But if anyone finds out about the letter, we shall all be in terrible trouble.'

Chapter 9 Messenger of the Gods

Before Lord Trimingham arrived, everyone at Brandham Hall had behaved in a very ordinary way. But now he was there, things seemed to change. We spoke with care and behaved less freely than before.

Mrs Maudsley planned something different every day. There were walks in the country. We had lunches or tea parties in the park. We travelled to interesting places. Mrs Maudsley made her suggestions after breakfast. They always sounded like commands to the rest of us. But to Lord Trimingham they were questions which were carried to him by one of her direct looks. He always agreed with her plans for the day.

I remember one of our trips very well. We were all sitting beside a stream. I enjoyed the meal and the cool drink from a bottle; but I hated all the conversation. I sat near Marian, but she did not look at me. She was interested only in Lord Trimingham sitting beside her, and I could not hear their conversation.

After a time Lord Trimingham looked up and said, 'Ah, there's Mercury!'

'Why do you call him Mercury?' Marian asked.

'Because he carries messages,' Lord Trimingham said. Turning to me, he said, 'You know who Mercury was, don't you?'

'I think he was one of the old gods,' I said.

'That's right. He was the messenger of the gods, too. He was their go-between.'

The messenger of the gods! I felt very proud. I was a traveller through heaven, visiting one god after another. It was like a wonderful dream – and it soon became a real dream. Lying on the bank of that stream, I went to sleep. When I woke up, I did not open my eyes immediately. Marian was talking to her mother.

'He doesn't enjoy these trips with us, Mother,' she said. 'He likes being alone.'

'Oh, do you think so?' Mrs Maudsley asked. 'He loves being with you, Marian.'

'And I love him,' Marian said. 'But he's only a child, Mother. We're not very interesting friends for him.'

'I'll have to ask him about that,' Mrs Maudsley said. 'When he comes with us, there are thirteen people; and thirteen is a difficult number. Marcus's illness is very unfortunate.'

'Yes. We may have to hold the dance at a later date,' Marian said.

'We won't change the dance,' said Mrs Maudsley. 'We can't disappoint all the people we've invited, can we, Marian?'

I did not hear Marian's reply, but I noticed again the disagreement between her and her mother. They never argued angrily in front of guests, but there were often clear differences of opinion between them. I opened my eyes then and stood up. Lord Trimingham was looking at me.

'Ah,' he said, 'Mercury is awake again. He has had a little rest.'

I smiled at him. There was something in his character that did not change. I always felt safe with him. His opinion of me would stay the same even if I made some mistake. Our little problems were not very important to him. He laughed at them, and he laughed at our jokes. No matter what happened, he was always calm.

When we went home that evening, I sat beside the driver. The conversation was easy. We understood each other perfectly. We talked only about facts, and I was very fond of facts. When I talked to the others at Brandham Hall, I could never discover the facts of the conversation. With them perhaps, it was the conversation of the gods! I was their messenger. And a messenger need not understand the messages that he carries.

Marian's suggestion that I should not go with them on these trips had annoyed me at first. But I remembered her words: 'I love him.' They were like a sweet taste in my mouth. Of course I enjoyed the drives through Norfolk, but Marian was right; there were things that I did not enjoy. I preferred the old huts, the swimming place and the haystack. I remembered then that beautiful plant, the deadly nightshade: *Atropa belladonna*. And I wanted to see it again.

'Do you know Ted Burgess?' I asked the driver.

'Oh, yes,' he said, 'we all know him.'

'Do you like him?'

'We're all neighbours,' he said. '*Mr* Burgess likes a bit of fun.'

I noticed that the driver said Mr Burgess. But I did not know why he used the word 'fun'. Ted Burgess did not seem to have much fun.

At last we came to the exciting part of the drive. There were two steep hills. We had to drive down the first and up the other.

At the bottom of the first we stopped. All the men got out in order to make the work easier for the horses. I asked the driver if I could get down, too.

'Why?' he said. 'The horses won't worry about your weight.'

I was not very pleased to hear that. But he helped me to get down, and I walked up the hill with the men.

Lord Trimingham was hot. He was wearing a white suit and a white hat.

'You look very cool, Mercury,' he said to me. 'This must be the hottest day of the summer.'

When we reached Brandham Hall I intended to read the thermometer, but this was impossible. Tea was ready, and there was a letter from my mother. I looked at the address proudly: Leo Colston, Brandham Hall, near Norwich. It was a good address.

I read the letter in my room, and it did not really interest me. At school I always enjoyed my mother's letters, but her news of home seemed unimportant now. I did not feel that I was a part of her life. My natural place was here, at Brandham Hall, I thought. Here I was a small god who carried messages for the other gods.

I tried to answer her letter, but the result was not a great success. I could not explain all the thoughts that were in my mind. I wrote about Viscount Trimingham, Marian and Marcus:

Viscount Trimingham called me Mercury because I carry messages for people. Marcus's sister, Marian, is still very nice to me, and I like her more than the others. I am sorry that she is going to get married. But she will then be a lady Viscount, and that will be wonderful.

I did not know why these thoughts made me feel important. And I was not sure that my mother would understand them.

I told her, too, that Marcus was not very well. But I did not say anything about a fever. She had said that I could swim; and I thanked her for this. It was not a very good letter, but I did not finish it until six o'clock.

I hurried away, then, to look at the thermometer. I expected something unusual, and I was not disappointed. The temperature was eighty-five degrees, but the little marker had been pushed up to ninety-four. Ninety-four! That was doubtless the highest temperature that had ever been reached in England. I wondered if it would reach a hundred tomorrow. It was my hope that it would.

All my thoughts seemed to lead to greater heights. I felt very excited, and I imagined that all my friends were excited, too. The high temperatures were only a part of the excitement. I was not quite sure about the events that would follow the dance, but they were connected with Marian and Lord Trimingham. Perhaps they would marry. There was pleasure in that thought, too. I would have to give up the part of me that found its happiness in her.

I heard a voice behind me. 'Are you enjoying yourself?'

Mr Maudsley had come to examine the thermometer. I answered him politely.

'Do you like hot weather?' he asked.

I said that I did. He started to move the markers. I did not want to watch him, so I said something quickly and hurried away.

Crossing a part of the garden, I heard another voice. It was Lord Trimingham's.

'Come here!' he called. 'We want you!'

I did not want to talk to anyone. I preferred to be alone with my own exciting thoughts, but he came to meet me.

'You're always walking about,' he said. 'Can you find Marian for me? We'd like her to play a game with us. I'm sure you know where to find her. You must bring her here alive or dead!'

I ran off. I did not know where she was, but I knew that I

would find her. I went round to the back of the house because that was the most interesting part to me. I ran down the path towards the old huts. I remembered that the deadly nightshade lived in one of them. Then I saw Marian. She was walking rather quickly up the path. When she saw me, she did not smile.

'What are you doing here?' she said.

We had stopped beside each other. There was more colour than usual in her face, and she was breathing quickly. I felt guilty for some reason, but I answered immediately. I thought she would be pleased.

'Hugh asked me to tell you . . .' I began, and then stopped.

'Yes? What did he ask you to tell me?'

'He asked me to find you . . .' I said.

I waited for her smile, but it did not come.

'But what did he say? Have you forgotten?' she asked.

It was the first time her voice had sounded unkind to me. My face probably showed that I was hurt. And she was different then.

'I know it isn't easy to remember everything,' she said. 'But what does Hugh want?'

'He wants you to play a game with them.'

'What time is it?' she asked.

'Nearly seven o'clock.'

'We don't have dinner until half past eight, do we? There's plenty of time. I'll go.'

We were friends again, and we walked back together. Then she said: 'We're going to have lunch with some neighbours tomorrow. Mother thinks you might not be interested. Do you mind staying here?'

'Of course not,' I replied. I remembered that this was Marian's idea, not her mother's, but it was not very important.

'What will you do to amuse yourself?' she asked.

'I'm not sure yet. I might do several things.'

'Tell me one of them.'

I had an idea then that she was guiding the conversation.

'I might play on a haystack. It's great fun.'

'Whose haystack?'

'Perhaps Farmer Burgess's.'

'Oh, his?' She sounded very surprised. 'Leo, if you go to his farm, will you do something for me?'

'Of course. What is it?' But I knew before she told me.

'Give him a letter.'

'I hoped you'd say that!' I said.

'Why? Is it because you like him?'

'Yes. But I like Hugh more, of course.'

'Ah, that's because he's a Viscount, perhaps.'

'Yes, that's one reason,' I said. I had real admiration for Hugh's title. 'But he's gentle, too. I thought a Viscount would be proud. And Mr Burgess is only a farmer.' I remembered his angry words to me at the haystack. 'He's a rather rough man, I think,' I added.

'Is he?' she said. 'I don't know him very well. We sometimes write notes to each other, on business. You said you'd like to take them.'

'Oh, yes, I would,' I said, excitedly.

'Is that because you like T– Mr Burgess?'

'Yes. But there's another reason.'

'What is it?'

This was my chance to tell her. It was not easy, but at last I said it.

'Because I like you.'

She smiled beautifully and said, 'That's a very sweet thought.'

She stopped suddenly. There were two paths in front of us. One of them went to the back of the house; the other led to the front.

'Which way are you going?' she asked.

'I'm going with you, to the front.'

Her face looked dark. 'I don't think I'll go,' she said. 'I'm tired.

Tell them that you couldn't find me.'

'Oh, no!' I cried. 'They'll be very disappointed.' I would be disappointed, too, because I had promised to bring her alive or dead.

'Then perhaps I should,' she said. 'But I'd like to go alone if you don't mind.'

I minded very much, but I did not tell her so. 'But you'll say that I sent you, I hope.'

'Perhaps I will,' she said.

Chapter 10 Secrets

The next day was Tuesday. Between Tuesday and Saturday I carried three letters from Marian to Ted Burgess. I brought back one note to her and two ordinary messages.

When he had read her first letter, he said, 'Tell her it's all right.' The second time he said, 'Tell her I can't fix it.'

He usually worked in the fields, and it was easy to find him. On Wednesday he was riding on a new machine. He stopped the horse and I gave him the letter. On Thursday afternoon another man was on the machine and Ted Burgess was looking for small animals to shoot.

I gave him the envelope, and he opened it immediately. I realized then that he had shot something. A thin stream of blood appeared on the envelope and on the letter. He had killed something before I arrived and the blood was still on his hands.

I cried, 'Oh, don't do that!' But he was so interested in the letter that he did not answer.

The next day I found him near the haystack, and he gave me the note.

'There's no blood on this one,' he said.

I laughed, and he laughed, too. I was not afraid of an animal's blood. I knew that hunting and shooting were part of a man's life. One day I hoped to enjoy those sports myself.

I had a lot of fun on the haystack. I played on it on each of the occasions when I took him letters. It was the best thing at Black Farm. Then, when I returned to the Hall, I did not have to tell a lie.

I said that I had been playing on Farmer Burgess's haystack.

◆

They were wonderful afternoons in another way, too. As the messenger of the gods I was very serious about my duties. Also, I was doing something for Marian which no other person could do. When she gave me the letters, she was excited then, even anxious. She was never excited when she was with Lord Trimingham.

I did not understand why the messages were important. And I did not know what they contained. Marian and Ted Burgess both said that they were 'business letters'. Perhaps Marian was helping Ted Burgess. Perhaps the letters contained advice which brought money to him. They might even contain cheques or pound notes, and that thought was exciting. Marian clearly had great confidence in me.

But I had never seen any money in the envelopes. The only things that Ted Burgess took out of them were short notes. Perhaps she wrote something that would be important to a farmer: something about the weather or the temperature, for example. I had not seen a thermometer at Black Farm. It had been eighty-three degrees on Tuesday, eighty-five on Wednesday and ninety-two on Thursday.

And then I had another idea. Ted Burgess might be in trouble, and Marian was trying to help him. I thought that perhaps the police were looking for him. This idea was the one I preferred; but it did not really satisfy me. If Ted was in trouble, he would show some sign of fear. When I delivered the messages, Marian and Ted were both excited and wanted to read them quickly. There was no sign of crime in the way they behaved.

Of course I did not intend to open any of the notes. I was too proud to do that and too anxious to please her. But there was another reason: the real story would probably be a disappointment to me. I was quite right about that.

◆

Friday was the day before the cricket match, and two things happened. The first was that Marcus got up. He was not allowed to go out, but Mrs Maudsley said that he would be well enough to watch the cricket match. I was very pleased to see him when he came to lunch. Although we were not great friends, we were about the same age. We shared some familiar thoughts, and I could talk to him without difficulty. We sat together, happily making jokes about each other, and had a great conversation. And then, during the meal, I suddenly thought of the difficulties.

If Marcus was with me, I would not be able to carry any more messages. Marcus would play on a haystack once or twice, but he would not want to do it every day. He did not like games as much as I did. I was Mercury, the messenger of the gods; but I could never tell Marcus that.

I could not give Ted Burgess a letter, or take a message from him, with Marcus beside me. In fact, he would not want to talk to the farmer at all, and he would criticize me if I did so. Marcus would certainly not go into the kitchen while Ted was slowly writing a letter.

The more I thought about the problem, the more difficult it seemed. Although I was used to lying to people, I did not want to lie to Marcus. It was not a question of right and wrong. I just did not want to lose a friend. At the same time, I loved the new feeling of adventure in my life. My services to Marian were now the most attractive part of life at Brandham Hall. By the end of the meal I had almost stopped talking to Marcus. Marian usually gave me the letters in the morning. But she had not given me one that day. After lunch, when Marcus and I were ready to run away, Marian called me.

I followed her to one of the rooms. She was sitting at a desk.

'Marian,' I said. I was going to tell her about Marcus and my difficulties. But there was a noise at the door. She quickly gave me a letter, and like lightning I pushed it into my pocket. The door opened, and Lord Trimingham came in.

'I heard you calling,' he said to Marian. 'I thought you were calling me. But it was this lucky young man. Can I take you away from him now?'

She smiled quickly and went to him.

When they had gone, I touched the letter in my pocket. I noticed immediately that the envelope was open. She had not had time to stick it down.

I found Marcus. I told him where I was going.

'Aren't you tired of that old haystack?' he said. 'It's too hot to climb haystacks today. Your suit will soon be very dirty, won't it?'

We argued a little. I asked him what he was going to do. 'Oh, I'll do something,' he said. 'I may sit and watch them spooning in the garden.'

We both laughed about that. We thought that spooning was stupid. Then a sudden thought gave me a shock.

'I'm sure Marian doesn't spoon with anyone,' I said, seriously.

'I'm not sure about that,' Marcus said. 'Some people think that she spoons with you.'

I did not like that, and I hit him. We fought for a few minutes until Marcus cried, 'Stop! You've forgotten that I've been ill.'

Pleased with my win, I left him. I hurried away to read the thermometer. It was three o'clock. The temperature was ninety degrees and might go higher. I hoped it would.

◆

I was halfway to Black Farm. I put my hand into my pocket and felt the letter again. With no other intention in my mind, I took it out and looked at it. There was no address on the envelope.

I thought about the customs and the laws at my school. If a boy left his letters on a table or a desk, anyone could read them. It was his own fault, and he could not complain. But no one was allowed to take another boy's letters from inside a desk or cupboard.

In school we often passed notes round. If the envelopes were open, anyone could read the letters. But an envelope that was stuck down contained a private letter; it should not be read.

The envelope of Marian's letter was open, and so I could read it. But still something stopped me. I was not sure if Marian had intended to leave the envelope open. She had stuck down all the other envelopes but had given this one to me in a great hurry.

At school we believed that facts were very important. Intentions were not important. A boy had either done something or he had not done it. A mistake made by accident was just as bad as a mistake on purpose. If Marian had made a mistake, she should be punished for it. But still I waited. She was not my enemy, like Jenkins and Strode. I was serving her, and her wishes were my wishes. I had to think about her intentions.

For a time I fought with this problem. Marian's face and figure came into my mind like a picture. Perhaps she had written something about me. If it was something kind, she would want me to read it.

I decided, then, to read it. There were other good arguments for doing this. This letter might be the last that I should deliver. If Marian was in danger, she would expect me to read it. But I did not take the letter out of the envelope. I read only the words that I could see. I knew already that three of them were the same.

I read only the words that I could see.

Dearest, dearest, dearest,

Same place, same time, this evening. But take care not to–

The rest of the letter was hidden by the envelope.

Chapter 11 Love Hurts

The letter was the worst disappointment of my life.

I felt that Marian and Ted Burgess had told me a terrible lie. They were in love! I had tried to explain the letters to myself, but I had never imagined that Marian and Ted Burgess were in love. I had been stupid, and I felt quite ashamed. At the same time I tried to smile.

They had lied to me without any difficulty at all. I had never expected that Marian would act in this way to me. She had been kind to me. She knew how a boy felt. She was my Virgin of the stars. I did not know how she could have behaved in this stupid way. If she had been a young servant, I would have understood the stupidity. We were used to young servants who cried about love. They came to the morning service with red eyes. But I thought Marian was different.

I remembered what Marcus had said about spooning. He was probably right. I had no doubt now that Marian and Ted Burgess liked to spoon. I understood now why the messages were secret: she was ashamed of them. I shared her feeling. I pushed the letter into the envelope and stuck it down.

But I had to deliver it to Ted Burgess.

When I left the shadow of the trees, my thoughts became brighter. The sun was warm and kind and seemed to forgive Marian. Perhaps it changed some of my ideas, too, because I was ready to forgive her.

I did not say, 'Spooning is a good thing because Marian does it.' I did not say, 'Other people mustn't spoon, but *she* can.' I was thinking of the other person. She could not spoon by herself.

I thought about Ted Burgess in a new way then, and I did not like the idea. But where was he? He was not in the field with the other men. I asked them where he was.

'He's at the farm,' they said.

'What's he doing there?' I asked.

They smiled but did not tell me.

I hurried there, thinking about the pleasure of the haystack. It was one fact in a lot of doubts.

Ted Burgess met me near the gate and greeted me politely. I noticed that his arms were browner than before. He looked so strong that I felt jealous. It was not easy to connect him with spooning or with any other silliness.

I gave him the letter. Turning away, he read it quickly and put it in the pocket of his trousers.

'Good boy,' he said. The words surprised me; and he added: 'You are a good boy, aren't you?'

'Perhaps,' I answered. Then I said, 'I won't be able to bring you any more letters.' I explained the difficulty about Marcus, and he listened sadly.

'Have you told her?' he asked.

'Who?' I was enjoying his disappointment.

'Miss Marian, of course.'

'No, I haven't,' I said.

'What will she say? We won't know what to do now, will we?'

I was silent for a moment. Then I said, 'What did you do before I came here?'

He laughed and said, 'It wasn't easy. But she likes you, doesn't she?'

'I think so.'

'And you want her to like you, don't you?'

'Yes,' I said.

'You don't want her to hate you, do you?'

'No.'

He came nearer to me. 'Why not?' he said. 'Why don't you want her to hate you? Where would you suffer?'

I felt that he had put a spell on me. 'Here,' I said, and I put my hand over my heart.

'Ah, you have a heart,' he said. 'I thought perhaps you hadn't.'

I was silent.

'If you don't take the letters, she'll be angry with you. You won't like that, will you?'

'No.'

'She depends on them, and I do, too. They're not ordinary letters. She'll cry, perhaps. Do you want her to cry?'

'No,' I said.

'It's easy to make her cry,' he said. 'You might think she was proud and calm; but she isn't. She used to cry, before you came here.'

'Did you make her cry?' I asked. I couldn't really believe that anyone would do that. And I remembered that she called him 'dearest'.

'I did, but I didn't do it on purpose,' he said. 'You think I'm a rough man. And perhaps I am. But she cried when she couldn't meet me.'

'How do you know?' I asked.

'Because she cried when she did meet me. Isn't that clear?'

It was not very clear to me. But Marian had cried, and the thought brought tears to my own eyes. I began to shake slightly.

He noticed this and said, 'You've walked a long way, and it's hot today. Come into the house.'

I did not want to go into the house. The kitchen was empty and uncomfortable. If we had an argument, that kitchen would give Ted an advantage over me. He was used to its ugliness, but I was not.

I tried to think of an easy subject of conversation. 'You aren't working in the field today,' I said.

'I was,' he replied. 'I came back to see Smiler. She's one of my horses.'

'Oh, is she ill?' I asked.

'She's going to have a baby.'

'Oh, I understand,' I said, but I did not understand. Babies were a great mystery to me. Several boys at school had claimed that they understood the facts about babies. They had offered to explain them to me. Perhaps Ted Burgess would explain them.

'Why is she having one?' I asked.

'It's natural,' he said. 'Horses have babies.'

'But does she want to have one if it makes her ill?'

'She hasn't any choice,' he said. 'She has to have it.'

'Why? What made her have one?'

The farmer laughed. 'She's been spooning,' he said.

Spooning! The word hit me like a blow. When horses spooned, the result was a baby. I could not understand it at all, and I felt quite ashamed.

'I didn't know that horses could spoon,' I said.

'Oh yes, they can.'

'But spooning is very stupid,' I said. 'And animals aren't stupid.'

'You'll understand when you're older,' he replied, quietly. 'Spooning isn't stupid. It's a word that people say when–' He stopped.

'Yes?' I looked at him.

'When they're jealous. They'd like to do it themselves.'

'If you spoon with someone, will you marry that person?' I asked.

'Yes, usually.'

'Can you spoon with someone without getting married?'

'Yes, perhaps,' he said.

'Can you be in love with someone and not spoon?' I asked.

He shook his head. 'It wouldn't be natural.'

Ted Burgess was fond of the word 'natural'. If something was natural, it was right. At least, that was what Ted believed. And now I understood that spooning was natural! I had never thought of that before. I had always thought that spooning was a kind of game.

'If you spoon with someone, will that person have a baby?' The question gave him a shock, and his red face became even redder.

'Of course not,' he said. 'What made you think that?'

'You did. You said that Smiler had been spooning. And that was why she was going to have a baby.'

'You're clever, aren't you?' he said. And I knew that he was trying to think of an answer. Then he said, 'Horses aren't the same as people.'

'Why aren't they the same?' I demanded.

He had to think hard again.

'Nature makes animals in a different way,' he said.

Nature again! His answer did not satisfy me. There was something that he had not told me; and I said so.

'That's enough questions for one day,' he said.

'But you haven't answered them,' I argued.

'And I don't think I will,' he said. 'You'll learn everything soon.'

'But if spooning is a nice thing–'

'Yes, it is nice,' he agreed. 'But you shouldn't do it before you're ready.'

'I'm ready now,' I said.

He laughed then, and his face changed.

'You're a big boy, I know. How old did you say you were?'

'I shall be thirteen on Friday the 27th.'

'Good. Well listen, here's what I'll do. I'll tell you all about spooning if you . . .' He paused then. I had already guessed what he was about to say, but he expected some help from me.

I said, 'Yes, if I . . . ?'

'If you go on carrying our letters.'

I agreed. The reason seemed clear to me now. I had learned a little about the force that drew Marian and Ted Burgess together. Although I did not understand it, I knew that it was strong. And its strength contained something beautiful and mysterious that I enjoyed.

Of course, I also wanted to find out about spooning; and I would not forget Ted's promise. I was sure that I could solve the problem of Marcus.

'You've forgotten something,' the farmer said suddenly.

'What?'

'The haystack.'

He was right. I had forgotten it. It seemed to represent something for which I had suddenly grown too old. I did not want to play.

'Play on that while I'm writing my letter,' he said.

Chapter 12 The Match Begins

I was disappointed with the temperature on Saturday. It was only seventy-eight degrees, and the sky was cloudy. They were the first clouds that I had seen at Brandham.

At breakfast everyone talked about the cricket match. A team from the Hall was going to play against a team from the village. Lord Trimingham was the captain of the Hall team.

'We haven't chosen our full team yet,' Denys said. 'We need one more man. Who is going to play?'

A few people at the table looked at me. I did not imagine that their looks meant anything.

'It's a difficult question, isn't it?' Lord Trimingham said.

'It is,' Denys replied. 'We shall have to reach a decision very soon. We must have eleven men.'

'What do you think, Mr Maudsley?' Lord Trimingham asked. 'We have to choose between two, I think.'

Lord Trimingham often asked his host for advice in this way, and it always surprised me. In other ways it seemed that Lord Trimingham, not Mr Maudsley, was the man of the house. But although Mr Maudsley almost never spoke, he never failed to answer a question.

'We had better discuss it in private,' he said, and all the men got up from the table and went into the library.

I waited outside in order to hear the result of their discussion. I had promised to take the news to Marcus because he was having breakfast in bed. I waited for half an hour before the men came out. Then I acted as if I was passing by accident.

'Ah, there's Mercury!' Lord Trimingham said. 'I'm afraid I have bad news for you, Mercury.'

I did not understand.

'We couldn't find a place for you in the team,' he said. 'Jim played last year' (Jim was a boy who worked in the house) 'and the year before. He plays well, too, and we had to include him. Miss Marian will be angry with me, but it wasn't my fault. You'll be our twelfth man.'

His speech was a great surprise to me. There was no disappointment in it. I felt so happy.

'Twelfth man!' I cried. 'So I shall be in the team! At least, I shall sit with them.'

'Are you pleased?' he asked.

'Of course! I didn't expect anything! Shall I go down to the field with you?'

'Yes.'

'Shall I get ready now?'

'Twelfth man!' I cried. 'So I shall be in the team!'

'You can, but the match is not starting until two o'clock.'

I was running to Marcus's room, but he called me back.

'Would you like to take a message?' he said.

'Oh, yes.'

'Ask Marian if she's going to sing "Home, Sweet Home" at the concert.'

When I found Marian, I did not think about Lord Trimingham's message.

'Oh, Marian, I'm playing in the match!' I cried. 'At least I'm twelfth man. I can help the team if someone breaks a leg or feels ill.'

'That may happen,' she said. 'Who would you like to have an accident? Denys, perhaps?'

'Denys?'

'No.' Perhaps I paused a moment before I said 'No'.

'You'd like Denys to be hurt,' she said in fun. 'But Brunskill would be better, wouldn't he?' Brunskill was one of the servants. 'He's a very old man. He'll break easily.'

I laughed at that joke. I couldn't imagine Brunskill running.

'Or Hugh?' she said.

'Oh, no, not him.'

'Why not?'

'Oh, because he was hurt before – and . . . and he's our captain, and I like him, and – oh Marian!'

'Yes?'

'He wants to know if you will sing "Home, Sweet Home" at the concert.'

'What concert?'

'The concert tonight, after the cricket match.'

The brightness left her face. She picked up some of the flowers that she was placing in a bowl. She held them up and looked at them.

'They're not very nice, are they?' she said. 'It's the end of July, of course. They don't like this hot weather.'

'It isn't the end of the month yet,' I said. 'Today is the twenty-first.'

'Is it?' she said. 'I've forgotten the days. There isn't enough time to think, is there? We have parties every day. Aren't you tired of them? Don't you want to go home?'

'Oh, no,' I said. 'Do you want me to go home?'

'I certainly do not. You're the best person here. I need you. How long are you going to stay?'

'Until the thirtieth.'

'That's very near. You can't go then. Stay until the end of the holiday. I'll speak to Mother about it.'

'I'll have to write to my mother–'

'Yes, of course. So that's all organised. And the flowers are ready, too. Will you carry the bowl for me?'

'Of course,' I said. 'But Marian–'

'Yes?'

'What shall I say to Hugh about the concert?'

She thought for a moment and then said: 'Tell him I'll sing "Home, Sweet Home". I'll sing it if he sings "The Flowers in Her Hair".'

I thought that was fair. I carried the bowl of flowers for her and then looked for Lord Trimingham.

I told him what Marian had suggested.

'But I can't sing,' he said.

He looked very unhappy about it. I wanted to say something that would make him feel happy. So I thought fast and then said: 'Oh, it was only a joke.'

'A joke?' he repeated. 'But she knows I can't sing.'

'That's why it's a joke,' I explained patiently.

'Oh, do you think so?' He smiled weakly. 'I wish I was sure of that.'

Later in the morning I saw Marian again. She asked me if I

had given Lord Trimingham her message. I told her I had.

'What did he say?' she asked.

'He laughed,' I said. 'He thought it was a very good joke. He told me he couldn't sing.'

'Did he really laugh?' she said. She seemed rather annoyed.

'Oh, yes.' I felt quite pleased. I thought that I had improved both the messages.

At lunch all the men were wearing white cricket clothes. It was not the usual kind of meal. Everyone stood up and took some food from the table. Marcus and I helped to carry dishes and plates. Then we had to wait for the others.

I remember my thoughts while we were walking to the cricket field. I hoped that we would win. It was very important that we should win. Winning was more important than any other thing. The members of the team were all equal now. The servants felt that they were equal to Lord Trimingham and to Mr Maudsley.

I received a shock when we reached the field. The team from the village had already arrived, and only a few of them had white cricket clothes. Some wore working clothes; others had blue or brown trousers. They did not have the smallest chance of success against us, I thought. If they were not dressed in the right clothes, they could not possibly play well.

Most of the men already knew one another. The others were introduced by Lord Trimingham. I shook hands with many people whose names I forgot almost immediately.

Suddenly I heard: 'Burgess, this is our twelfth man, Leo Colston.'

Without thinking, I stretched out my hand. Then I saw who it was. My face felt hot and red, and Ted looked surprised, too.

He said quickly, 'Oh, yes, my lord. We know each other. He comes to the farm and plays on my haystack.'

'Of course he does,' Lord Trimingham said. 'He told us. You

should make him carry messages, too, Burgess. He's an excellent messenger.'

'I'm sure he can do many things,' the farmer said.

Lord Trimingham turned away, and Ted and I were left together.

'Are you the captain of the team?' I asked. I could not imagine Ted in any lower position.

'Oh no,' he said. 'I don't know much about cricket. I just hit the ball. Bill Burdock is our captain. He's over there.' And Ted pointed to a man who was talking to Lord Trimingham. 'Look, they're deciding who should play first,' he said. We played first.

The game had already started when the ladies arrived with Marcus. I was annoyed by their lateness.

'It's quite simple,' Marcus said to me, quietly. 'They just refused to leave.'

He went with the ladies to a row of chairs. I sat with our team.

I have never watched a cricket match since that day at Brandham. I know now that it was not an ordinary local game. Lord Trimingham's family had always loved cricket, and Mr Maudsley continued the custom. There was a big wooden board which showed the score. Two men wrote the details on large cards, and we each had our own card. The edge of the field was marked by a white line. All these things were correct, and so they satisfied me.

Many people had come from Brandham and from other villages to see the game. Most of them wanted the team from the village to win, although they also welcomed our men. But in my mind they were all enemies that we had to defeat. I particularly wanted Lord Trimingham to succeed. He was our captain, and I admired the word 'captain'. I liked him, partly because he stood for the greatness of Brandham Hall and I enjoyed that greatness very much. Our score was 15 when Lord Trimingham played. He played beautifully for a short time but added only 11 to the score.

When he came back, everyone clapped him. Marian clapped louder than anyone else. Her eyes were bright when she looked at him. He tried to smile at her. I wondered if she was secretly laughing at him. Her happiness might be just another joke.

More trouble followed. We lost three more men, and our score was 56. Then it was Mr Maudsley's turn. He walked slowly on to the field. He was then about fifty years old and looked to me like the figure of Father Time. I thought that he was clearly too old to play cricket. He reached his place and studied the positions of the other team. Bill Burdock and his men moved closer to Mr Maudsley. I felt very sorry for him and I waited sadly for his return.

But he did not return. He stayed on the field, and the reason is quite clear to me now. The qualities that had brought him success in business also brought him success in cricket. And the chief of these qualities was the quality of judgment. Sometimes he hit the ball, and sometimes he didn't seem to move at all. He used his strength carefully.

When Denys went on to the field, the score was 103. Mr Maudsley had made 28 of these. Before he went out, Denys had told us his plans.

'Father will get tired if he runs a lot,' he said. 'I shan't let him run. I'll either hit the ball to the edge of the field or leave it alone.'

For a time these plans succeeded. Denys hit the ball twice to the edge, but he and his father did not play well together. Mr Maudsley always wanted to take a fair chance; but Denys often stopped this. At last Mr Maudsley refused Denys's sign. He shouted, 'Come on! Run, man!' The words seemed to hit Denys on the back. He ran, but it was no use. He was not fast enough. Denys walked back with a red face.

Mr Maudsley now controlled the game. Although I was pleased with his success, at the time something seemed wrong with it. Mr Maudsley was clever, and he had excellent judgment. But these, I thought, were not really the right qualities for success in sport. I believed that strength and skill should defeat brains.

We quickly lost the rest of our team, but Mr Maudsley was not beaten. He scored 50, and our total was 142. When the men came in, there was loud clapping for Mr Maudsley. Everyone stood up, and Lord Trimingham shook hands with him. We had tea then and discussed the game. Mr Maudsley said very little. At five o'clock our team went on to the field. The village had two hours in which to defeat us.

Chapter 13 The Twelfth Man

The village lost five of their men quickly. Their score then was less than 50. The match became less interesting, and I began to feel sorry for the village team. My attention moved to the trees behind the field. There was a big cloud above them. The cloud was moving very slowly towards the sun. Soon it would reach the sun, and then . . .

There was a noise behind me. Ted Burgess was going out to play. I was not sure if I wanted him to score a lot for the village. My thoughts had been quite clear until now; I wanted only our team to play well. But Ted Burgess was different. I wanted Ted to do well. I wanted him to fight, and I hoped that he would fight hard.

He had a few narrow escapes, and then he began to score. He scored 4, 8, 10. He then hit the ball so hard that it fell in the trees. That knock added 6 to his score. A few minutes later he hit another ball to the edge. Ted's score was now 20, and someone shouted, 'Good old Ted!'

I cannot quite remember when Ted's score began to worry me. It reached 40 and then 50, and he was still playing. Ted's 50 was very different from Mr Maudsley's. There was no judgment or care; it was just luck. But I knew that many wins are the result of good luck. I was worried and pleased at the same time.

Marian was sitting just below us, and there was an empty chair beside her. I went down to her and whispered: 'Isn't it exciting?' When she did not answer, I repeated the question. She turned her face to me, and I understood. She was too excited to speak. Her eyes were bright, her face was red and her lips were moving slightly. I was a child and usually lived with children; I knew the signs. The effect of the game on Marian was so strong that I felt it myself. As time passed, my feelings became clearer to me: I hoped that the village would win. I knew that she hoped so, too.

I looked at the score. Two men still had to play, and the village needed 21 in order to beat us. The crowd was silent. Ted Burgess was still on the field. He hit the ball straight towards us. One of our men ran to stop it, but it was moving very fast. It struck his hand hard, and he could not hold it. Mrs Maudsley jumped up with a cry. Marian put her hands in front of her face. For a moment we were all confused. But neither of the ladies had been hit, and they both laughed at their escape. The ball lay at Mrs Maudsley's feet. I threw it to the man who had tried to stop it. He did not pick it up. His face showed his pain, and he was holding his left hand in his right.

Lord Trimingham examined the man's hand, and there was a discussion on the field. Then they walked off the field, and Lord Trimingham said: 'We've had an accident. Pollin' (that was the man's name) 'has hurt his thumb. He'll have to leave the field, and so we need our twelfth man.'

My knees were shaking when I walked out with Lord Trimingham.

'Ted Burgess is annoying,' he said. 'We've got to beat him. Now, Leo, you stand there. Sometimes he hits on this side, and this is where you can help us.'

I felt weak and anxious. Five minutes ago I was sitting beside Marian. Now I was playing in the match. It was a very sudden change.

The game continued, and for a time no one scored. I began to feel calm. Then Ted hit the ball twice to the edge, adding 8 to his score. The village team now needed only 11 in order to win.

Ten minutes later their last man came out to play, and they needed only 7. There was almost complete silence from the crowd. Lord Trimingham now had the ball, and Ted was getting ready to play.

It was a strange situation: the farmer against the lord. But also Marian was in a strange position. She stood for the Hall, but she seemed more loyal to Ted Burgess.

There was another great knock to the edge, and the crowd shouted for Ted. The village had now scored 140 and needed only 3 more to win. Lord Trimingham ran up with the ball. Ted's face and body turned, and he hit the ball hard. It travelled towards me in almost a straight line. Ted began to run and then stopped. He stood and watched me.

I stretched my arm above my head. The ball stuck in my hand, but the force of it knocked me down. When I stood up, I was still holding the ball. I heard the sound of clapping. Lord Trimingham came towards me. I have forgotten what he said. But I remember one thing: his speech of thanks was a speech given to a *man*.

As my friends and others came over to me, I felt very happy. But in one way I was sorry. I had made the catch which finished Ted Burgess. And I wanted to tell him that I regretted it. I hoped that he still thought of me as a friend.

I went to him and said: 'I'm sorry, Ted. I didn't really mean to catch that ball.'

He stopped and smiled. 'That's a kind thought,' he said. 'It was a wonderful catch. I never thought our messenger would do that to me!'

The ball stuck in my hand, but the force of it knocked me down.

The clapping for Ted was very loud. He was clearly the favourite of the crowd. Even the ladies were interested as we walked past. All except one. I noticed that Marian did not look up.

I looked at the score card. Ted Burgess had scored 81.

Chapter 14 Leo's Second Test

After the match there was a supper and concert in the village. The hall was specially decorated for the occasion. Many local people were present, and both teams were invited. The colours, the flags and the heat all made me feel excited. The food was good, and everyone was very happy.

After supper Mr Maudsley made a long speech. This surprised me because he rarely spoke at home. It was quite a clever speech, too. He managed to name and to say kind words about almost every man who had played in the match. I hoped that my name would be included, and I was not disappointed.

'Lastly,' he said, 'I must thank Leo Colston, our twelfth man. Although he was the smallest man on the field, he defeated one of the greatest.'

Everyone looked at me. Ted was sitting almost opposite me, and he smiled warmly. He was wearing a dark suit and a high collar. He never seemed to look natural when he was dressed in good clothes.

The speeches continued, but at last someone said: 'Now let's have a song.' And there were general cries of agreement.

The end of the hall was higher than the rest of the floor. On this platform there was a piano, with a small seat in front of it. But now I heard some whispering. The piano player was not there. Then someone explained: he was ill and had sent a message, but for some reason no one had received the message.

There was great disappointment. A cricket match and a supper were not complete without songs and it was still early; the whole evening stretched in front of us. We already had a piano and just needed a piano player. Lord Trimingham looked at the faces around him, and everyone looked away.

Then suddenly someone moved. Marian stood up, walked quickly to the piano and sat down. She was wearing a pale blue dress, and she looked very beautiful.

The members of the cricket teams sang first, and soon it was Ted Burgess's turn. But Ted did not seem to hear when his name was called. He did not move from his place.

'Come on, Ted!' his friends shouted. 'We know you can sing!'

Lord Trimingham spoke, too. 'Don't disappoint us, Ted,' he said. 'We didn't have to wait for you on the cricket field, did we?'

Everyone laughed then, and at last Ted stood up. He was shaking slightly as he walked to the piano. He was carrying a number of pieces of music under his arm.

The arguments had not seemed to interest Marian. When Ted reached her, she looked at him. She said something to him, and he gave her the music. Ted's first song started badly. Then, slowly, his voice became stronger, and he sang well. Everyone clapped loudly and asked him to sing again. He thanked everyone and left the piano. The clapping then was louder than ever. The crowd liked his attitude and wanted more. At last they succeeded.

The new song was a love song. It is probably not known now, but I knew it and liked it. And I liked the way Ted sang it.

'When other lips and other hearts
Their thoughts of love shall tell . . .'

The others enjoyed it, too. I knew a lot about other lips and other hearts which told their thoughts of love. The sounds of the words were like the sounds of a poem. For Marian and Ted

Burgess the poem had a power which I could not understand. Although I did not understand it, I believed in it. I did not know then that love might ever cause unhappiness. It was a good subject, I thought, for a song or a poem. It was certainly not connected with spooning. At the end of Ted's song there were tears of happiness in my eyes.

Everyone clapped Marian and Ted loudly. She smiled at him, but he did not do anything. People laughed, and the man who was sitting beside me said: 'What's the matter with Ted? He's usually more polite to the ladies than that. It's because she's from the Hall, of course.' But at last he smiled at Marian and thanked her. The man next to me said, 'That's better. She's a lady, I know, and Ted's a farmer. But they look well together, don't they?'

When Ted came back to his seat, he seemed annoyed. Everyone noticed this and enjoyed it. It added some fun to the party. Ted at a concert was just as popular as Ted on the cricket field. The crowd laughed at him as much as they had clapped for him before.

Other songs followed, and Marian showed us her skill at the piano. And then, during a pause, Lord Trimingham said: 'Now it's our twelfth man's turn. Can't you sing something, Leo?'

After all these years it is not easy to remember my exact thoughts at that moment. Before the concert I had played in my first cricket match against men. That was my first test, and I had passed it. Now they wanted me to sing at a public concert. And I knew that I could succeed in this second test, too. I did not know that on my birthday there would be a third test. And I certainly did not know that my failing the third test would change my life completely. I went to Marian at the piano.

She said, 'What are you going to sing, Leo?'

'I haven't any music,' I said.

She smiled at me, and I can still remember that wonderful smile. She said, 'Perhaps I can play for you without the music.

What's the name of the song?'

I told her.

'It's my favourite song,' she said. 'I don't need the music.'

While I was singing, people were silent. That was a good sign. It meant that they were enjoying the song. But the clapping really surprised me. It seemed to shake the roof of the hall.

The people clapped for half a minute. They wanted another song. Marian was still sitting at the piano, and I went to her side.

'They want me to sing again,' I said.

'Do you know any other songs?' she asked.

'I know "Angels ever bright and fair", but it's a religious song.'

She smiled again, but said: 'I don't know it. I can't play it for you.'

I was very disappointed because I wanted to hear the clapping again. Our conversation must have been heard by other people.

A voice said: 'Is it "Angels ever bright and fair"? I think I've got the music for that.' A man walked to the piano, carrying a book of songs.

I loved that song, and I sang it for Marian. I imagined that she was flying with me in Heaven:

'Angels! Ever bright and fair,

Take, oh take me to your care . . .'

Marian stayed at the piano, and I received the clapping alone. But it did not stop. She got up then and took my hand. She smiled at the audience, and she smiled at me.

After my success I returned to my seat. I was still excited by the angels ever bright and fair.

Ted looked at me and said: 'You sang very well. No one could have sung that better than you did. It was perfect. I thought that I was in church.'

That seemed to be the problem now. After my religious song, the party became quiet. It was late, and I felt tired. Perhaps I slept for a short time. The next thing I heard was Marian's voice. She was singing 'Home, Sweet Home'. She had a beautiful voice, and the words of the song were beautiful too. I remembered that Lord Trimingham had requested that particular song. It was probably not Marian's favourite.

She refused to sing again. The clapping that rang through the hall had no effect on Marian. The harder we clapped, the further away from us she seemed. I was not annoyed about this, and the crowd did not seem to be disappointed either. She was not like the rest of us. It had been a wonderful day and evening. Everyone felt satisfied with their good fortune.

On the way home Marcus talked about my success. I wondered if he was feeling jealous of it.

I said, generously, 'You could do as much, or more perhaps.'

'That's true,' he said. 'On the right occasion I would try not to look like a sick cow.'

'On what occasion?' I demanded.

'When you were singing, you looked just like a sick cow. And you sounded like one, too. I was sitting beside Mother, and we almost had to laugh.'

These words were perhaps not very serious, but they made me angry.

'If you weren't a poor, sick boy, with legs like a bird's, I would knock you down.'

'Yes, yes, I know,' he said. 'I didn't really feel ashamed of you. We were grateful. You beat that man, Burgess, for us. When I saw him at the piano with Marian, I felt ill.'

'Why?' I asked.

'You'd better ask Mother,' he said. 'She hates the people from the village. Did you notice the smell in the hall?'

'No.'

'Didn't you? It was terrible. And then you sang that song about the angels; and that was terrible, too. I thought Burgess was going to cry. I couldn't guess Trimingham's thoughts because of his face.

But he told Mother you were wonderful.'

We were nearly at the house. Marcus paused for a moment and then said quietly: 'Can you keep a secret?'

I promised that I would tell no one.

'I'll tell you then, though Mother made me promise not to tell anyone. Marian's going to marry Trimingham. Everyone will be told at the dance. Are you glad?'

'Yes,' I said. 'I am. I'm sure I am.'

Chapter 15 The Fifth Viscount

On Sunday morning my friends continued to discuss my successes. I had won the cricket match for the Hall. My singing had been the best at the concert. I could not wish for kinder words than I received.

But I was also pleased for Marian because she was going to marry Lord Trimingham. I could not imagine a better marriage. She was the most wonderful girl in the world, and he was the ninth Viscount Trimingham. It was an important relationship, and it would have an effect on my life at Brandham Hall. Marian and Ted Burgess would not ask me to carry any more messages.

I felt glad and sorry about the messages. Marcus was well again and I could not explain the letters to him. But I enjoyed the adventure and the dangers. I liked Ted Burgess, too. Although he was only a farmer, I admired his strength. At the same time I was jealous of him. He had some power over Marian that I did not understand. In one way we were in competition, but we were also good friends. And on that Sunday morning I was not worried by thoughts of Ted Burgess.

I am old enough now to know why. I had beaten him twice in fair competition. On the cricket field I had made the catch which vanquished him. And at the concert my songs had enjoyed greater success than his. Ted Burgess had been totally defeated, and so he did not worry me.

I had almost forgotten his haystack, too. I agreed now with Marcus that haystacks were for young children, not for big boys. I even felt a little ashamed of it. Marcus and I could now enjoy the rest of the holiday. We could practise our own private fun. I felt quite sure that Marian would now forget Ted Burgess. I knew nothing about such relationships at that time, but one thing seemed certain even to me. When a girl agreed to marry a man, she stopped writing love letters to another man. That was natural and right; no one could argue about it. My duties as Marian's messenger had been the most attractive part of life at Brandham Hall, but that did not seem to be true now. I did not think of Lord Trimingham as serious competition. I did not see him as an ordinary person; he was on a different level. I wished for Marian's happiness. If she was happy, I would be happy too. Happiness was a simple thing, I thought. If you wanted something, you tried to get it. And when you got it, you were happy. I was sure that Marian wanted to get Lord Trimingham. When she married him, she would also get his house. Marcus had told me that. And when he married her, he could afford to live at Brandham Hall. Marcus said that Marian would have a lot of her father's money.

After breakfast I wrote a long letter to my mother. I told her all about my successes. I also told her that Marian had asked me to stay another week. I wrote: 'Please let me stay. I hope that you are not lonely without me. I have never been happier than I am now, except with you.'

I posted the letter and then waited near the door. The people who were going to church were not yet quite ready. I wondered what I should do in the afternoon. I thought of Ted and remembered his promise to me: he was going to tell me all about spooning. I had been very anxious to hear that, but now I did not particularly want to hear it. I would let him tell me, but not today. Next week, or the week after, I would go and say goodbye to him.

As we were leaving the house, I noticed the clouds. I had already seen the thermometer, and the temperature was rising. It was going to be another hot day.

I soon felt tired of the service and became bored with the priest. I thought about the Trimingham family, whose history was written on the wall. I had a special interest in it now because Marian would soon be a member of the family. Marcus had told me that she would be a Viscountess. And wives, I noticed, were included in the names on the wall. 'Caroline, his wife' and 'Mabel, his wife' were two of them. I imagined another: 'Marian, his wife' but I did not want to think about that. I felt sure that neither of them would ever really die. But even if they did, there would always be someone with the name Trimingham. I imagined then the ninety-ninth Viscount Trimingham, and then the hundredth. The idea of their unbroken history, for century after century, was a very serious thought.

But it *had* been broken once. I remembered that the fifth Viscount was missing from the list. I wondered what had happened to him. I decided to ask Lord Trimingham about it.

My chance came after church. Lord Trimingham was again last in the line. I thought that Marian would wait for him. She did not, and so I did.

'Hello, Mercury,' he said.

'Can I take a message for you?' I asked.

'No, thank you,' he replied. 'I don't think there will be many more messages.' His voice sounded perfectly happy.

'She didn't leave her book in church today,' I said.

'No, she didn't. But have you ever known a girl who forgets things as she does?'

'I haven't,' I replied, 'but she plays the piano very well.'

'Yes, and you sing very well,' he said.

I had expected this. And it was easy then to ask: 'Why is there no fifth Viscount?'

'No fifth Viscount?' he repeated. 'What do you mean?'

'In the church. The fifth Viscount Trimingham is missing from the list.'

'Oh, yes,' he said. 'I didn't know you meant him. I'd forgotten his number.' He was silent then.

'Why isn't he in the list?' I demanded.

'It's a sad story,' Lord Trimingham said. 'He was killed.'

'Oh,' I cried, feeling excited. 'In battle, I expect.'

'No, not in battle.'

'Was it an accident?' I asked. 'Was he climbing a mountain, or trying to save somebody?'

'No,' he answered. 'It wasn't really an accident.'

I knew that he did not want to tell me. Perhaps I was wrong to continue questioning him, but I was excited by my successes and decided to go on.

'What was it?' I asked.

'He was killed in a fight with another man,' Lord Trimingham said.

'Oh, that's *fun*!' I cried. 'What had he done? Did he fight for his good name?'

'Yes, he did, really,' Lord Trimingham said.

'Had someone been rude to him? Had he been called a thief or something?'

'No,' Lord Trimingham said. 'He fought about another person.'

'Who?'

'A lady. She was his wife.'

'Oh.' I felt disappointed. I had an idea that the business had something to do with spooning. But I tried to be interested and asked: 'What had she done?'

'He thought that she loved another man.'

'Was he jealous?' I asked.

'Yes. It happened in France. The two men fought, and the fifth Viscount was killed,' said Lord Trimingham.

'That was unfair, wasn't it?' I said. 'The other man deserved to die.'

'Yes, that's probably true. The Viscount was buried in France.'

'Did the Viscountess marry the other man?' I asked.

'No, but she stayed abroad. The children came to live in England, except the youngest. He stayed with her in France.'

'If the lady hadn't been the Viscountess,' I asked, 'would he have fought?'

'But she *was* the Viscountess,' he replied.

'Yes, of course. But if they were only planning to get married, would he have felt the same?'

Lord Trimingham thought about this. At last he said: 'Oh, yes, I think so.'

So it seemed that the fifth Viscount's position was not very different from Lord Trimingham's. But I tried not to think about it. Marian was going to get married. I felt sure that she could not love Ted Burgess at the same time.

I said, 'Was he angry with *her*, too?'

'I don't think so,' Lord Trimingham answered.

'But wasn't it her fault as well as the man's?' I asked.

'Nothing is ever a lady's fault; you'll learn that,' he replied.

These words had a great effect on me. I knew immediately that he was right.

'Was the other man a very bad man?' I asked, although I didn't really believe in badness.

'Several ladies had loved him,' he said. 'He was young and strong. He was a Frenchman.'

'Oh, a Frenchman,' I said. That seemed to explain everything.

'Yes, and he could shoot straight. I don't think he was a particularly bad man. People were different then.'

'But would it be really bad if it happened now?'

'Yes. He would be a murderer now, at least in England.'

I tried to imagine the scene of the fight. It was probably a lonely place with cups of coffee and two guns. The men's friends measured the distance: fifty steps. Someone gave the sign. The men shot at each other. One man fell.

'Did the fifth Viscount bleed very much?' I asked.

'I don't know. This sort of fight is not legal in England now.'

'But men can still shoot each other, can't they?' I asked.

'They shot me,' he answered, trying to smile.

'Yes, but that was in a war. Do men still shoot each other about ladies?'

'Sometimes,' he said.

'And then they're murderers, aren't they?'

'Yes,' he replied.

We had caught up with Marian. Lord Trimingham noticed her and said: 'Ah, there's Marian. Shall we go and talk to her?'

Chapter 16 Leo's Tears

I still remember that conversation with Lord Trimingham. He had said that no matter what happened, nothing was ever a lady's fault. The more I thought about the idea, the more generous it seemed.

After lunch Marcus said to me, 'I'm sorry I can't play with you this afternoon.'

'Oh, why not?' I asked. I felt quite disappointed.

'I'm going to visit our old nurse, Nannie Robson, who lives in the village. She isn't very well. Marian asked me to stay with her for the afternoon. Marian said that she's going there, too, after tea. What are you going to do? You're not going back to that old haystack, are you?'

'Oh no,' I replied. 'I'm tired of that. I might go for a walk.'

But first I went to see the thermometer.

On my way I thought about Marian's kindness to her old nurse. She had been very kind to me. And now I knew that she was also kind to old or poor people. She really was a wonderful girl.

The temperature was eighty-one degrees; that was three degrees higher than it had been yesterday. The marker was still rising. I hoped that it would reach eighty-five during the afternoon.

My thoughts returned to Marian. I wondered what present she was going to take to Nannie Robson: a cake, perhaps, or a bowl of soup. And then a voice behind me made me jump.

'Hello, Leo! You're the man I'm looking for.'

It was Marian, but she was not carrying a cake or a bowl of soup. She was carrying a letter.

'Will you do something for me?' she said.

'Oh yes. What shall I do?'

'Just deliver this letter.'

'Who to?' I asked.

'Who to?' she repeated. 'To the farm, of course.'

I was very surprised. Many thoughts rushed into my mind, but only one stayed there. It was a terrible thought. Marian was going to marry Lord Trimingham, but she was still in love with Ted. And I knew what the result of that might be: somebody would be murdered. I felt really frightened and cried out: 'Oh, I can't!'

'Why can't you?' she asked.

This was difficult to answer. I knew the secret of her letters to Ted Burgess. I knew that she was going to marry Lord Trimingham. I should not have answered at all, but I was very frightened. I believed that somebody would die; and this fear made me answer her.

'It's because of Hugh,' I said.

'Hugh?' she repeated. 'What do you mean?'

'He might be worried.'

She came nearer and stood over me. Her eyes looked very angry.

'This is not Hugh's business,' she said. 'Only Mr Burgess is interested in it. Do you understand, or are you a stupid boy?'

I was so frightened now that I could not say a word.

'You are a guest in our house,' she cried. 'We have welcomed you and been kind to you. And when I ask you to deliver a letter, you refuse! I'll never ask you to do anything for me again. Never! I won't speak to you again!'

I tried to stop her angry words. I put my hands up to push her away, or perhaps to bring her closer. She almost hit me in her temper. I am sorry now that she did not.

Then suddenly her expression changed, and she became very calm.

'Oh, I know your trouble,' she said. 'You want me to pay you, don't you?' She opened her bag. 'How much do you want?'

I had suffered enough. I took the letter and ran away as fast as I could.

I was used to criticism from other people. But Marian was different. In my ordinary life she had helped me in so many ways that I would miss her kindness. She had not laughed at my clothes when I first came to Brandham. She had bought me all my new clothes. It was because of her that I had enjoyed the greatest success at the concert.

But she was also the queen of my private thoughts. She was my Virgin of the stars! As I ran further from her, my sadness increased. I understood now that she did not really love me. She had seemed fond of me so that I would carry messages between her and Ted Burgess. Her kindness was not real.

The shock of this discovery made me stop running, and I began to cry. Crying helped my disappointment. I crossed the

She almost hit me in her temper. I am sorry now that she did not.

river. There was no one in the field. It was Sunday, of course. I would have to go on to the farm.

I remembered then all the ways in which Marian had used me. She had told her mother that I did not enjoy the trips and the parties. She wanted me to go to Black Farm instead! For the same reason she had asked me to stay an additional week at Brandham and had organized it with her mother. For the same reason she had sent Marcus away today. It was not kindness to their old nurse, Nannie Robson. She had asked him to visit the old lady so that he could not go with me to the farm! I even believed that she had played the piano at the concert for Ted Burgess!

I cried again, although I could not hate Marian. I remembered Lord Trimingham's words: 'Nothing is ever a lady's fault.' It was a very happy thought. But the trouble must be somebody's fault. I wondered whose fault it was. And I thought it must be Ted's fault.

I soon arrived at the gate of Ted's farm. I walked past the haystack and knocked at the kitchen door. There was no answer, so I went in. Ted was sitting at the table. He was holding a gun between his knees.

'Hello,' he said. 'I'm glad to see you.' He rested the gun against the table and looked at me. 'Have you been crying?' he asked. 'Your eyes are red. Has somebody been cross with you? It's some woman, probably.'

I started crying again then. He took a clean cloth out of his pocket and dried my eyes. I did not stop him. I knew that tears would have no effect on Ted's opinion of me.

'I must do something to make you happy,' he said. 'Would you like to see Smiler and her young one?'

'No, thank you,' I said.

'Would you like to play on the haystack? I've put some more hay at the bottom.'

'No, thank you.'

He looked round the room. 'Would you like to use my gun?' he asked. 'I was going to clean it, but I can do that later.'

I shook my head. I did not want to agree with anything that he suggested.

'Why not?' he said. 'You *must* learn how to use a gun. This one will hurt your hands a little, but it's not like a cricket ball! Ah, I haven't forgiven you yet for making that catch.'

When he talked about the cricket ball, I became more interested in his suggestion.

'Come outside,' he said, 'and I'll shoot something.'

I could not continue refusing, so I followed him outside. I thought that shooting was probably a slow business, but I was wrong. As soon as we were outside, Ted lifted the gun to his shoulder.

The noise frightened me. I watched the bird as it turned slowly in the air. It landed just in front of us.

'That one won't eat from my fields again,' he said.

He picked up the dead bird and threw it into some trees. The other birds flew away.

'Do you ever miss?' I asked.

'Oh yes, sometimes. Now, would you like to watch while I'm cleaning the gun?'

I felt a lot better when I went back into the kitchen. Ted poured some oil on a piece of cloth and then cleaned the gun. When he had finished, he gave the gun to me. I held it up, pointing it at several things in the room. Then I pointed it straight at Ted.

'You mustn't do that!' he cried. 'You must never point a gun at anybody.'

I quickly gave the gun back to him.

'I'll make you a cup of tea,' he said. 'But I'll have to boil some water first. Just wait here a minute.' He went out of the kitchen.

He returned suddenly and said, 'Have you brought a letter for me?'

I gave it to him. I had forgotten it.

'Have you any message for Marian?' I asked.

'Yes,' he replied, 'but do you want to take it?'

The question surprised me. I thought I was going to cry again.

'No,' I said; 'but if I don't, she'll be very angry.'

'Was it Marian who made you cry?' he asked. I did not answer and he continued: 'We should give you something. A messenger should be paid. What would you like?'

I should have answered 'Nothing'. But Ted seemed to have put a spell on me again. He was not angry with me. Our conversation was perfectly natural. I wanted to please him. I did not refuse his payment as I had refused Marian's money. And suddenly I remembered something.

'You promised to tell me something,' I said.

'Did I?'

'Yes. You promised to tell me all about spooning.'

'Yes, I remember,' he said. 'But wait. I think the water is boiling.' He left the kitchen but soon came back.

'I enjoyed your singing at the concert,' he said. 'You sang just like a bird.'

'I practised those songs at school,' I said. 'We have quite a good teacher.'

'I didn't go to school for long,' Ted said. 'When I was a boy, my mother took me to a big church in Norwich. The singing was wonderful. One of the boys had a voice just like yours. I've never forgotten it.'

I had the idea that Ted was trying to change the subject.

'Thank you,' I said; 'but you were going to tell me about spooning.'

He moved the cups on the table. 'Yes,' he said. 'I don't think I will tell you now.'

'But you promised!' I cried.

'I believe that you already know all about it,' he said.

'I don't, I don't,' I cried. 'But you promised to tell me.'

There was a pause. Ted looked down at me. Then he said: 'It means putting your arm round a girl and kissing her. That's all.'

'I know that,' I cried, feeling very angry. 'Everybody knows that. But spooning means more than that. What else does it mean?'

'It makes you feel very happy,' he said. 'What do you like doing best?'

I was annoyed because I could not answer the question immediately. I had to think first. Then I said: 'I like doing the things that happen in dreams: flying or . . . waking up suddenly after a bad dream. I've dreamed that my mother is dead. Then I wake up and she's still alive.'

'I've never had that dream,' he said. 'But it's the right idea. Think of it, and then add something to it. That's what spooning is like.'

'You haven't really told me anything,' I said.

'I have told you,' he said patiently. 'It's better than the thing you like best.'

I was too angry to notice how angry he was.

'Describe it for me,' I cried. 'You know, but you won't tell me. I won't take any more messages for you if you don't tell me.'

But Ted had had enough of me. He stood beside me, as hard and straight and dangerous as his gun. I saw the temper in his eyes.

'Go,' he said. 'Go quickly, or you'll be sorry.'

Chapter 17 An Important Decision

BRANDHAM HALL,
NEAR NORWICH,
NORFOLK.

Dear Mother [I wrote],

I am sorry to tell you that I am not enjoying myself here. Please, Mother, send me a telegram. Say that you want me to come back. You can say that I must be at home on my birthday. That's on Friday, 27th July, so there is still plenty of time. If a long telegram is expensive, just say: 'Please send Leo back. I will write and explain.' I don't want to stay here, Mother. The people are very kind to me, and I like the place, but I am tired of the messages.

I paused then. I should explain the messages, but how could I? They were secrets.

I could not tell my mother about them, but I could use other arguments to make her understand how I felt. I continued my letter.

The farm is two miles away. I get very tired in the Great Heat [my mother was fond of saying 'in the great heat'; she hated hot weather]. I have to go to the farm nearly every day. They seem to depend on the messages. When I don't want to take them, they are angry.

I paused again. I could also write about questions of right and wrong, and this might influence my mother. When I did something wrong, she described it as either Rather Wrong or Very Wrong. I did not believe that anything was wrong, but my mother did, and so I wrote:

I think that these messages are Rather Wrong. They may even be Very Wrong. I am sure that you would not like me to carry them.

I hope you are quite well, Mother. I would be very happy if I did not have to carry these messages.

Your loving son,

LEO.

When I had finished the letter, I felt much better. In one afternoon I had twice run away from angry people. I had run out of Ted's house as fast as any boy could run. When I reached the gate of the farm, I looked back. Ted was waving and shouting at me. I thought he intended to run after me. So I kept on running until I was on land that belonged to Brandham Hall.

I quite expected that Marian would tell everyone about our argument and that I was a stupid, ungrateful boy. I imagined that no one would speak to me, but I arrived for tea at the usual time and everyone was kind to me. Mrs Maudsley was not there. Marian was at the head of the table, and she seemed very happy.

Her success in this duty was different from her mother's. Mrs Maudsley had always organized the meal. Her guests seemed to eat and drink following her orders. But Marian amused us. We laughed at each other, and we all enjoyed the occasion. Lord Trimingham was sitting beside her on a low chair. We could see only his head, but everyone could see her. It was a picture of the future, I thought.

Marian poured a cup of tea for me. She looked straight at me and said: 'Three sugars, or four, Leo?'

'Four, please.' I said it on purpose. I hoped that the other guests would laugh. And they did.

I thought of Ted's lonely tea at Black Farm. His kitchen was like the home of some wild animal. Here, I was in a rich, comfortable house. Tea at Brandham was an exciting experience. I enjoyed it more, perhaps, because I knew Ted's poor home.

Later, Marian looked at me again. Although she did not speak, there was a clear message in her eyes. It was 'I want to talk to you after tea. Stay here when the others leave. Or look for me.'

But I did not stay there, and I did not look for her. I went to my room, locked the door and wrote the letter to my mother.

I had decided to leave Brandham. If I left, the messages between Marian and Ted would have to stop. If there were no messages, Marian would not be able to meet Ted. She would have to stop loving him.

I had once liked being their messenger, but now I hated it. It was wrong. I was anxious to cause problems between Marian and Ted. I wanted to stop their love.

As I was going to post the letter, Lord Trimingham called me.

'Would you like to do something for me?' he said.

'Oh, yes!'

'Find Marian, please.'

I felt weak. I did not want to see Marian at all.

'But you told me that there would not be any more messages!' I said.

He seemed to be annoyed. I thought he was going to be angry.

'Oh, don't worry, then. I wanted to say something to her. She's going to London tomorrow, and I may not have another chance.'

'Is she going to London? She hasn't told me about it,' I said.

'She's very busy,' he said. 'Please try to find her.'

I suddenly remembered a great excuse. 'Marcus told me that she was going to visit Nannie Robson after tea.'

'Marian is always at Nannie Robson's!' he cried. 'She says that the old lady can't remember anything now. She even forgets if Marian has visited her or not.'

I ran away then, but Lord Trimingham called me back. 'Don't run far in this heat,' he said. 'You look pale. I hope you're not going to be ill. We don't want two sick people in the house.'

'Oh, who's the other one?' I asked.

'Mrs Maudsley. But you'd better not talk about it.'

I wondered why I should not talk about it. Perhaps the family did not want the other guests to know that Mrs Maudsley was ill.

'Is she *very* ill?' I asked.

'No, I don't think so,' he said. He seemed sorry then that he had told me about it.

I wondered if she was just saying that she was ill. People sometimes did that when they were annoyed. Perhaps Mrs Maudsley wanted Marian to go to London, but Marian did not want to go. At Brandham differences of opinion were usually between Marian and her mother.

Chapter 18 Lovers in the Garden

On my way out of the house I met Marcus. He asked me where I was going.

'Shall we go and see those old huts again?' I asked. 'We can look at the deadly nightshade.'

'Ah, yes, the belladonna.'

'Atropa belladonna,' I said. I could not often correct Marcus. But when he gave me a chance, I always took it.

The huts were at the end of the garden. We had to walk about half a mile. There were trees on both sides of the path. Sometimes the darkness there frightened me. Perhaps that was why the place attracted me. But Marcus was with me now, and I did not feel afraid.

Suddenly Marcus stopped. 'Look at that footprint,' he said.

We bent down and examined the ground.

'I think it's a woman's footprint,' I said.

'Or a thief's,' Marcus said. 'I'll tell Mother that we've seen a strange footprint on the path. She's afraid of thieves.'

'Is she?' I asked. 'I thought she was very brave. I'm sure she's

'I think it's a woman's footprint.'

braver than my mother.' I could not believe that Mrs Maudsley was afraid of anyone.

'Oh, you're wrong,' he said. 'She's often frightened. It's almost like an illness. She's ill now. She's so worried that she becomes ill.'

'What's worrying her?' I asked. 'The servants do all the work, don't they?' It was the housework that always worried my mother.

He shook his head mysteriously. 'It's Marian,' he said.

'Marian?' I repeated. 'But why?'

'Mother isn't sure that Marian wants to marry Trimingham.'

That news surprised me. I had never imagined that she would not marry him. I was also surprised that Marcus had told me. I wondered if he knew or had any idea about Marian's secret. If he knew anything about it, then of course his mother knew it too.

A sudden thought came into my mind. 'Did you see Marian at Nannie Robson's house?' I asked.

'No,' he replied. 'She hadn't arrived when I left. The old lady was disappointed. She said that Marian rarely came to see her.'

'Lord Trimingham told me something that Marian had said. She said that Nannie Robson couldn't remember anything. She couldn't even remember Marian's visits.'

Marcus laughed. 'That's not true,' he said. 'Nannie Robson's memory is better than mine. It's about four times better than yours!'

I hit him then, but the news worried me. Perhaps Nannie Robson was right, and Marian rarely visited her. If that was true, then Marian was lying to almost everyone.

I said: 'Lord Trimingham also told me that Marian is going to London tomorrow. Why is she going?'

'She's going to buy some new clothes for the dance. That's one reason. But she's mainly going because of you.'

'Me? Why?'

'She's going to buy a present for you,' he said.

'A present!' I cried. For a moment I was sorry about my argument with Marian. 'But she has already given me many presents.'

'This is a special one for your birthday,' Marcus said loudly and clearly. 'You'll never guess what it is.'

'Do *you* know what it is?' I asked.

'Yes, but I promised that I wouldn't tell you,' he said. 'And now I've got to break that promise. Promise that you won't tell anyone.'

'I promise,' I said.

'It's a bicycle.'

Bicycles are very common now, and most children have one. But in the year 1900 they were unusual. I wanted a bicycle more than any other thing, but I never expected to have one. My mother would never be able to afford the money. I questioned Marcus about the details.

'I haven't seen it,' he replied, 'and Marian has to go to London to buy it. But I can tell you one thing that you haven't asked me.'

'What?'

'Its colour.'

'What colour is it?'

'It's green. And do you know why?'

I could not guess.

He began to laugh. 'Because you're green yourself of course! Marian said that green is the best colour for you.' He danced round me, crying, 'Green, green, green.'

I felt angry and disappointed. At school the word 'green' meant silly or stupid and Marian probably knew that. My green suit was also a present from her. All my pleasure left me.

'Did she really say that?' I asked.

'Yes, yes!' he cried. He danced round me again.

For a moment I hated Marcus, and I hated Marian. I decided to hurt both of them.

'Do you know where Marian is now?' I asked.

Marcus stopped and turned to me quickly. 'No,' he said. 'Do you know where she is?' He was suddenly very interested.

'Yes, I know.'

This was quite untrue. I did not know *where* she was. But I guessed that she was with Ted.

'Where, where?' he said.

'Not far from here,' I replied.

At that time I did not guess why Marcus was particularly interested. But the reason is quite clear now: it was a piece of news for his mother. Perhaps they had both had doubts about Marian's stories of her frequent visits to Nannie Robson.

My attack on him and his sister made me feel better. It helped improve my temper. At the same time I believed that I had not really hurt Marian. I had only *said* I knew where she was.

We had continued along the path, and the huts were quite near now. Suddenly I saw something which made me shake. It was the hut where the deadly nightshade grew. And the deadly nightshade was coming out of the door! The tree had grown so much that the hut could not hold it.

We stopped at the door and looked in. Marcus wanted to push past the branches and go inside. 'Oh, don't go in,' I whispered. He smiled and stayed beside me. From that moment we were friends again. We forgot our argument.

The tree had grown to a great height because there was no roof on the hut. Some of the branches had grown higher than the walls. The leaves and flowers filled every empty space. Its beauty was almost too dangerous to look at.

This plant had flowers and fruit at the same time. It was a very strange plant. Although I was afraid of it, it still attracted me. I thought that it held some guilty secret. I was very interested in

Its beauty was almost too dangerous to look at.

every kind of secret. Perhaps that was why I loved it.

It was getting dark. The effect of the deadly nightshade was so strong that I did not want to leave the place. But at last I turned away from the hut. And at that moment we heard the voices.

One of them was just a very faint sound, but I recognized the other immediately. It was the voice which had sung at the concert:

'When other lips and other hearts
Their thoughts of love shall tell . . .'

Marcus did not recognize the voice. It was gentle but also urgent. It demanded something but was also happy to ask for it.

Just then the second voice became clearer, but it was not clear enough for us to recognize it.

Marcus was very excited. 'There's a girl, too,' he whispered. 'They're probably spooning. We must tell them to go.'

The suggestion really frightened me. I knew that Marian and Ted were there. I did not want to see them at all, and I did not want them to see me, either.

'No,' I whispered. 'Don't interrupt them. That wouldn't be polite, would it? Let's leave them alone.'

I started walking back along the path. Marcus followed me, but he still seemed annoyed.

'They're on our land,' he said. 'Why have they come here to spoon? I think I'll tell Mother.'

'Oh, don't tell her,' I said quickly. 'Promise you won't, please.'

But he refused to promise and probably told her that night.

We walked on towards the house. I thought about many things. I thought of the fight that the fifth Viscount had fought in France. I remembered the footprint which we had seen on the path. It was Marian's footprint of course.

Then I thought about the green bicycle! If Marian intended to hurt me, I would accept the unkindness and I would accept the bicycle, too. It was already better than all my other things. If I went home before my birthday, I would not get it. Mrs Maudsley and Marian would be annoyed and would probably send it back to the shop. Perhaps they would give it to Marcus, although he already had one.

I imagined the scene when I arrived home with my bicycle. Everyone would admire it. I had not learned to ride a bicycle yet, but my mother could soon teach me. And then I could ride up and down the hills . . .

But I was not very happy about it. The bicycle was a kind of payment because I knew something about her secrets. She hoped that I would not tell them to anyone.

I left Marcus at the door of his room. There was plenty of time before dinner. So I ran down the stairs and looked into the letter box. The letter to my mother was still there. I touched the door of the letter box, and it opened. The letter was in my hand. If I tore it up, I would have the bicycle. If it was posted tomorrow, I would lose the bicycle. It was a moment of great decision.

I pushed the letter back into the box. And I went to my room, feeling very unhappy.

Chapter 19 The Lady-Killer

In the morning I looked at the letter box. It was empty. All the letters had gone to the post office. I felt very glad.

Marian and Mrs Maudsley were not at breakfast. Marian had gone to London by an early train, and her mother was still in bed. I wondered again about her illness. Marcus had said that her troubles made her ill. I thought that she always seemed very calm. But I was still afraid of the light from her dark eyes when she looked at me. She had always been kind to me, kinder, perhaps, than Marian had been. But even if she had been my mother, I would not have been brave enough to love her.

I did not know if Marian loved her. They watched each other like two cats. But then they also turned away from each other, as cats do. It was not my idea of love. I decided at the time that they had no confidence in each other at all. Everything seemed easy or natural when Mrs Maudsley was absent. I was glad, too, that Marian would be away until Wednesday. I expected my mother's telegram by then, and I was ready to leave. I already felt that I was not a part of Brandham.

Marian had been everything that I most admired. I loved the way she spoke my name. She had put a spell on me, but it was not just the spell of her beauty. It was mainly, perhaps, her quickness of mind. She seemed to know our thoughts before we spoke them. She often answered questions a moment before they were asked, but she never made people feel uncomfortable.

Until yesterday I had loved Marian, but now all my thoughts of her were poisoned. She had always thought that I was green. Marcus had said so. Perhaps it was a lie, of course, but I did not think of that at the time, so I was glad to see her empty chair at breakfast. Today and tomorrow were going to be easy days, without arguments and unkind words.

Four of the other guests had left with Marian. So we were only seven at breakfast: Mr Maudsley, Lord Trimingham, Denys, Marcus and myself, and Mr and Mrs Laurent. The cats were away, and the rest of us were very glad.

After the meal we did not discuss any plans for the day. There were no messages, no problems. We were all wonderfully free!

◆

That day and the next no one visited Brandham Hall, and we did not leave it. I now had time to look around the whole house. On Monday the temperature was eighty-three degrees; on Tuesday it was eighty-eight. I hoped that it would soon reach a hundred.

'Marian will be very hot in London,' Lord Trimingham said. 'The heat in those shops is terrible.'

I imagined the scene: Marian was in a busy bicycle shop. Everything was covered with oil. 'Oh, there's some on my skirt. What shall I do? It's a new skirt, too. I've only just bought it,' she would say. She would laugh and make the girls in the shop laugh too. Then, when she came out of the shop, she was followed by a small green bicycle, ready for the road.

A green bicycle! It was a lovely thought, but there was an ugly thought beside it. If Marcus had not explained the bicycle's colour so unkindly, I would probably not have posted the letter to my mother.

At breakfast on Tuesday there was a letter by my plate. I did not recognize the writing. It was posted at the village of Brandham. I could not imagine who had written it. Only two people wrote letters to me: my mother and my aunt. I waited anxiously for the end of breakfast. When at last we left the table, I hurried to my room.

BLACK FARM
Sunday

Dear Mr Colston,

I am sorry that I sent you away from the farm. It has been worrying me. I didn't intend to send you away. I was ashamed to tell you the things you wanted to know. Perhaps when you are older, you will understand the difficulty. I was wrong to lose my temper, as I do sometimes.

I ran after you to say sorry. Perhaps you thought that I wanted to catch you. Although you may not want to come again, I'd like to see you. Can you come next Sunday at the same time? If you come, I'll try to tell you.

Please believe that I am sorry for my temper. And try to forgive me.

Your good friend,
TED.

I read the letter several times, and I almost believed that Ted meant it. But people had lied to me before. He wanted me to go on carrying the notes. The letter had come too late to have any effect. I still wanted to know the real facts about spooning, but next Sunday I planned to be at home with my mother.

There was one sentence in the letter that I was not sure about: *I was wrong to lose my temper, as I do sometimes.* I decided to ask Lord Trimingham about it.

I found him in a room which was called the smoking room. The men went there to smoke after meals.

'Hello,' he said. 'Have you started smoking?'

'No,' I said, 'but I'd like to ask you a question. Do you know anything about Ted Burgess?'

'Yes,' he said. 'Why?' He seemed surprised.

'I was wondering about him,' I said.

'Are you still thinking about the cricket match? You caught that ball very well,' Lord Trimingham said. 'But Ted is quite a good man. He's a bit wild, of course.'

'Wild?' I repeated. I thought of lions. 'Do you mean that he's dangerous?'

'He's not dangerous to you or to me. He's a lady-killer, but that isn't a big problem.'

A lady-killer: what did that mean? I did not think that Ted would kill Marian. I had been afraid of a man-killer, but that fear did not exist now. The danger would end as soon as I left Brandham Hall.

'What else can I tell you about him?' Lord Trimingham asked. 'He's got a quick temper. He's had a few fights.'

At that moment Mr Maudsley came in. Lord Trimingham rose, and I stood up too.

'Sit down, Hugh, please sit down,' Mr Maudsley said. 'Has this young man started smoking already?'

Mr Maudsley smiled at me. I did not say anything.

'We've been talking about Ted Burgess,' Lord Trimingham said. 'I told Leo that Ted was a lady-killer.'

'Some people think so, I believe,' Mr Maudsley said.

'It's his own business, of course.' Lord Trimingham looked at me quickly. 'I've been talking to Ted about the army. He'd be a good soldier. He has no wife or family, and he shoots well, too. I spoke to him yesterday, at the farm. But I'd suggested the army once before. I'm not a very good advertisement for it, am I?'

He was talking about his face, of course. He wanted us to believe that it did not worry him.

'What did he say?' Mr Maudsley asked.

'At first he wasn't interested. But yesterday he asked a lot of questions.'

'Do you think he'll join?' Mr Maudsley said.

'He may. I'll be rather sorry if he does. He's a good man.'

'The area won't miss him much,' Mr Maudsley said.

'Why not?' Lord Trimingham asked.

'Oh, there's one quite good reason,' Mr Maudsley answered.

There was silence then. I had not understood all the conversation, but I felt worried by it.

'Is Ted really going to the war?' I asked.

'He probably will,' Lord Trimingham said.

I left the smoking room then. As I was shutting the door, Mr Maudsley said to Lord Trimingham: 'Somebody told me that he had a woman here.'

I did not quite understand that either. Perhaps Mr Maudsley was talking about the woman who cleaned Ted's house.

Chapter 20 One Last Message

I expected my mother's telegram on Tuesday morning, but by lunchtime it had not arrived. My letter to her probably arrived late. I still hoped to leave Brandham on Thursday.

Marcus and I were now good friends again. He had stopped feeling jealous of my success. During the day we walked in the park and we talked about school. We fought once or twice. He told me many secrets. Although I did not agree with this terrible habit, I enjoyed the news.

He told me about the dance. It was going to be wonderful. He took a programme from his pocket and showed it to me. It was a list of dances. In the middle of the list there was the word 'DINNER'.

'Who will give the news about Marian and Lord Trimingham?' I asked.

'We may not give it at all,' he said. 'We may just let it *spread*.'

'Oh!' I was very disappointed.

'It will spread quickly,' he said. 'But you and I will be in bed. We'll have to go to bed at twelve o'clock. You are really too young to be awake after ten o'clock. And do you know what else you are?'

'No,' I said.

'Don't get angry, but you're a little green. *Green*. Do you understand?'

I hit him, and we fought again.

I knew, of course, that I would not be at the dance. I enjoyed the conversation because it seemed unreal. The dance had rather frightened me because I was only just learning the skill and I could not turn very well. But I liked to imagine the dances.

Marcus then told me about the plans for my birthday. They were a complete secret, he said. When I heard the details, I began to worry. I was sorry about my plan, too, because everyone was going to give me something. The green suit and my other new clothes had not been real birthday presents. And of course there would be a birthday cake too.

We had reached the road to the village. A boy on a red bicycle was coming towards us.

'A telegram!' we both cried. Marcus waved to the boy. He stopped and got off his bicycle. I felt sure that the telegram was for me; and I stretched out my hand for it.

'Maudsley?' the boy asked.

'*Mr* Maudsley,' Marcus corrected him. I put down my hand and watched Marcus's face. I wondered about his reaction to the news. I was still sure that the telegram was from my mother.

Marcus opened it. 'It's only from Marian,' he said. 'She's coming back by the late train tomorrow. Now let's go to the village.'

I had been wrong. My mother could not afford to send a telegram. She had written a letter, and it was going to arrive tomorrow. So I had another day in front of me. Although I was still at Brandham Hall, my heart was already at home.

But the letter did not come on Wednesday morning. I was surprised but not very worried. Letters were also delivered to the Hall at teatime. And I felt certain that it would arrive then. I wondered how I could spend the day. It was already very hot. I hoped that the temperature would go up to a hundred degrees.

This was going to be my last day at Brandham. If they wanted me to stay until Friday, I would agree. Perhaps they would give me the presents before I went to the station. I hoped they would. At least, I wanted the bicycle, but I couldn't have the cake of course.

When I was going away to school, my mother used to ask two questions: 'Have you forgotten anything, Leo?' and 'Is there anyone you should *thank*?' Tomorrow I intended to thank everyone who I should thank. There were Marian, Marcus, Mr and Mrs Maudsley and the servants. I imagined myself thanking them.

I remembered Ted. He had not given me very much, but he had written to me. He was probably going to fight in the war, and that thought still worried me. I should say goodbye to him.

But first I had to lose Marcus. I could not say goodbye to Ted if Marcus was with me. I had an idea.

'Ted Burgess promised to give me a swimming lesson,' I said quickly. This was not true, but I had heard many lies and lying is like a fever, it spreads to other people. 'I won't be away very long,' I added.

'Are you going to leave me alone?' Marcus said in fun.

'You left me,' I argued, 'when you went to Nannie Robson's.'

'Yes, but that was *different*. She's my old nurse, but Burgess is . . .' I did not know the word that Marcus used, but it sounded bad. He did not like Ted. Actually, he did not like any of the people from the village.

I took my swimsuit and went down to the river.

There was one field which still needed attention. Ted was working there. I did not go to him. This was my last visit to the farm, so it was a special occasion. Ted must come to me. He was driving the machine, and at first he did not see me. Then one of the men told him that I was there. He stopped the machine and began to walk towards me. I went to meet him.

Before we reached each other, we both stopped.

'I didn't think you'd come again,' he said.

'I came to say goodbye. I'm going away tomorrow or Friday.'

'Goodbye, then, Mr Colston, and good luck,' he said.

I looked at him. He seemed strange and different. I remembered when I had first seen him in the river. He had looked as powerful as some wild animal. But now he looked tired and weak. He was probably about twenty-five years old. His face now seemed a lot older than that.

'Is it true that you are going to the war?' I said.

'Why?' he asked. 'Who told you?'

'Lord Trimingham.'

He did not answer.

'Do you know that Marian is going to marry him?' I asked.

'Yes.'

'Is that why you're going to the war?'

'I'm not sure that I *am* going,' he said. 'She hasn't said anything yet. I'll go if she wants me to go. My wishes aren't important.'

I thought that was the speech of a weak man. And now, after fifty years, I still think so.

'You haven't told anyone about us, have you?' he said suddenly. 'It's only business between me and Miss Marian, but . . .'

'I haven't told anyone,' I said.

'She said you wouldn't tell. But I said, "He's only a boy. He might talk." '

'I haven't told anyone,' I repeated.

'We're both grateful to you,' he said. 'Not many boys would carry those messages for us. I'm still sorry I shouted at you on Sunday. Every boy wants to know those things, and I was wrong not to tell you. I know it was a promise. I'll tell you now if you like. But I'd rather not–'

'Don't worry about it,' I said. 'I know someone who'll tell me. I know several people who'll tell me.'

'I hope they won't tell you the wrong things,' he said anxiously.

'How can they? Everyone knows the same things, don't they?'

'Yes, but I'd be sorry . . . Did you get my letter? I wrote on Sunday and posted the letter that night.'

'I got it on Tuesday morning,' I said.

'Good.' He seemed pleased. 'I don't write many letters, except on business. But I felt so sorry that I had to write to you.'

Tears came into my eyes. I managed to say 'Thank you'.

'You said you were going tomorrow.'

'Yes,' I said, 'tomorrow or Friday.'

'We may meet again,' he said.

He came close to me and stretched out his hand. 'Goodbye.'

'Goodbye, Ted.'

I turned away from him and then turned back.

'Shall I take one more message for you?'

'That's very kind,' he said. 'Do you want to take one?'

'Yes, just one more.' It could not hurt, I thought. I wanted to show him that we were friends.

'Tell her that tomorrow is no good,' he said. 'I'm going to Norwich. It will be Friday, at half past six.'

I promised to tell her. I looked back once. Ted was looking back, too. He took off his hat and waved it at me.

Chapter 21 The Cats Return

Mrs Maudsley was not at tea on Wednesday. She was probably worrying about my birthday party. I would be worried, too, if there was no letter from my mother. I did not want to attend the dance. The long list of dances had frightened me, and Marcus had seemed to enjoy my fear. But my troubles soon turned to happiness. My mother's letter lay on the tea table. I did not hurry to open it. I wanted to wait a little before enjoying the pleasure the letter would give me. I had to tell Mrs Maudsley about it before too long, but I hoped to wait a little before that, too. I believed that she would hate my leaving Brandham.

My darling boy,

I did not send you a telegram, and I hope you were not disappointed. I hope, too, that this letter won't disappoint you.

Your two letters came at the same time, and at first they confused me. In the first letter you said that you were very happy. You asked if you could stay another week. I felt very proud of your successes. Then, in the second letter, everything was different. You said that you were not enjoying yourself and you wanted to come home. I thought that you had changed your opinion very suddenly. In the morning you were happy. In the evening you were unhappy. I wondered what had happened in those few hours. You said that you didn't like taking the messages. But you enjoyed the work before. Why is it different now? You would be an ungrateful guest if you refused to do this small service.

You said that the messages might be wrong. How can they be wrong? You told me that everyone was kind and good to you. I can't imagine that they would want you to do anything *wrong*. Perhaps it would be rather wrong if you refused to go. I'm sure they wouldn't be angry with you. They would wonder what kind of home you have.

Of course the great heat is difficult, I know. Perhaps you should explain to Mrs Maudsley that you feel tired sometimes. [My mother thought that I was Mrs Maudsley's messenger.] Ask her *very nicely* if one of the servants can take the messages. I am sure that she will say yes.

Please try not to be disappointed about this. It would be a mistake if you left suddenly. I think your hosts are good people. They will be very nice friends for you when you grow up.

I think we should be *patient*, Leo. The ten days will soon pass. You are like me: sometimes sad and sometimes happy. A few months ago you were unhappy at school. Do you remember? Some bigger boys were unkind to you because you used a long word. But you soon forgot about it and were happy again. I hope that you are already feeling better.

Goodbye, dear boy. I shall write again before your birthday. I'll send you a little present. I'll keep the real present until you come back. Can you guess what it is?

With all my love,

MOTHER.

Grown-up people often refuse a child's request. When this happens, the child cannot do anything. My mother had refused my request, and I could do nothing about it. I knew that I could not talk to anyone. In me lay the bones of a dead secret. But was the secret really dead? No, it was not. It was alive and dangerous and might even kill someone.

Soon I decided to leave my room. I had to stay at Brandham Hall, so I must get used to the place again. I walked around at the back of the house, and then went outside. I ran behind the long grass and trees and soon reached the front of the house. I could hear voices there. And I wondered if Marian had come back.

I did not want to be alone with her because she was the main cause of my unhappiness. Ted had frightened me more than she had. But she had hurt me more. I understood men and boys. I knew how they behaved. Schoolboys know everything about each other's characters. They are not polite in order to hide their real thoughts. Ted was like a schoolboy. He was angry at one moment and then suddenly kind. He did not admire me particularly, and I felt the same about him.

But I *had* admired Marian. In fact, I had loved her. In a way she had been as kind as my mother was. Both of them had now turned against me. I could forgive my mother because she did not know what she was doing. But Marian did know.

So I hoped not to see her. Of course, I had to see her at meals, and I had to give her Ted's message. I controlled the business between Marian and Ted. Without the messages, they could not meet. If they did not meet each other, there would be no danger. I was not going to take any more messages.

The next day was Thursday. Mrs Maudsley appeared at breakfast and greeted me with kind words. She was sorry, she said, that she had not given attention to one of her important guests. She had been quite unable to leave her room. I looked at her, but I could see no signs of illness. Her look was still sharp and direct. We did not feel as comfortable as we had felt for the past three days. After breakfast, as Marcus and I were going out, he whispered to me: 'The cats have come back.' I knew that he was talking about his mother and Marian. I was going to reply, but we heard a voice behind us: 'Marcus, I want Leo to help me for a moment.' It was Marian, and I followed her.

She asked me how I had enjoyed myself without her. I said, 'Very well, thank you.' I thought that was a safe reply, but it did not please her.

She said, 'Those are the first unkind words you've said to me.'

I had not intended to be unkind. I wondered how to show that I was sorry. 'Did you enjoy yourself?' I asked.

'No,' she replied. 'I missed Brandham very much. Did you miss me?'

I hesitated for a moment. I did not want to say the wrong thing again.

She noticed this and said: 'Don't say "yes" if it isn't true.'

I answered then: 'Of course I did.' It was not true, but I wished it was.

'I expect you played with Marcus,' she said. 'Did you have fun?'

'Yes. I'm sorry you didn't enjoy London.'

'You're not at all sorry,' she said. 'You wouldn't worry if I was killed in an accident. You've got a heart of stone. And all boys are the same.'

I did not like the conversation very much, and I was confused, too. Was Marian serious, or was she trying to make a joke?

'Are men the same?' I asked. 'I'm sure Hugh isn't like that.'

'Why do you think he isn't?' she asked. 'You're all exactly the same: stones, big pieces of stone. You're all as hard as the beds at Brandham.'

I laughed. 'My bed isn't hard,' I said.

She was silent then. I thought that she was unhappy. Perhaps I knew why she was unhappy now.

'Is Ted really going?' I asked.

'Going where?' she said. 'What do you mean?' Her voice sounded surprised, but I didn't really notice it and went on: 'Is he really going to the war?'

Her mouth opened, and she looked straight into my eyes.

'To the war?' she repeated. 'Who said he's going to the war?'

I had never imagined that she might not know. Then I remembered that Lord Trimingham had spoken to Ted on Monday. Marian was in London then. But it was too late to change the subject.

'Hugh told me,' I said. 'Hugh asked him to become a soldier. And Ted said that he might.'

'Hugh!' she cried. 'Hugh! Do you mean that Hugh has talked Ted into becoming a soldier? Do you really mean that, Leo?'

I was frightened. But I knew that she was not angry with me.

'Hugh said that he'd spoken to him about it.'

'Oh!' she cried. 'Hugh *made* Ted say that he'd go.' Her face was white, and her eyes were like dark holes in a piece of ice.

'No,' I said. 'That's not right. Hugh couldn't *make* him do anything, could he? Ted's stronger than Hugh.'

'You're wrong,' she said. 'Hugh is much stronger than Ted.'

I could not understand that at all. It was just not true. But a new look came into Marian's face. She was still angry, but she also looked afraid.

'Did Hugh say *why* he wanted Ted to go?' she asked.

'Yes. Because Ted wasn't married, and he had no family. He also said that Ted shoots well.'

Marian's face changed again. 'He shoots *very* well,' she said. 'Oh, yes, he does. Hugh wouldn't do that. I won't let him.'

She went on, almost wildly: 'I'll soon stop it! I'll make Ted stop it! Ted's a dangerous man when he's angry. I won't let him go. I'll tell Hugh–' She stopped suddenly. 'A few words would be enough.'

'What words? What will you tell him?' I demanded.

'I won't marry him if Ted goes to the war. I'll tell him that.'

'Oh, you mustn't!' I cried. I imagined the fifth Viscount's body, dead on the ground. 'Hugh doesn't *know*, Marian.'

'What doesn't he *know*?' she asked.

'He doesn't know about the messages.'

'He doesn't *know*,' she repeated. 'Then why does he want Ted to go to the war?'

'Oh,' I said in surprise. 'It's because he's a soldier himself. And he loves his country. And he wants the army to be strong. That's why he spoke to Ted.'

'You may be right,' she said. 'If you're right, then Ted is silly. And I shall tell him that.'

'Why is he silly?' I asked. The description did not seem right, and I was trying to defend Ted.

'Oh, because he is. Why should he have to listen to Hugh?'

'Perhaps he *wants* to go!' I said.

'Oh, he couldn't!' she cried.

I thought she was afraid for Ted. But I know now that she was really thinking of herself. I asked a question that had been in my mind for a long time. It was a rather stupid question.

'Marian, why don't you marry Ted?'

For a moment her face showed all her unhappiness. 'I can't, I can't!' she cried. 'Can't you understand?'

'But why are you going to marry Hugh if you don't want to marry him?'

'Because I must marry him,' she said. 'You don't understand. I've got to marry him.' Her lips shook and she began to cry.

I remembered my first days at Brandham when Marian had helped me. I forgot that she had lied to me. I forgot that she had called me 'green'. We cried together for several minutes.

Then she looked up and said: 'Did you go to the farm while I was away?'

'No,' I said, 'but I saw Ted.'

'Did he give you a message for me?'

'Yes. He said he was going to Norwich today. It would be Friday at six o'clock.'

'Are you sure he said six o'clock?' she asked.

'Quite sure.'

'Not half past six?'

'No.'

She kissed me then. She had never kissed me before.

'Will you still be our messenger?' she asked.

'Yes,' I whispered, but I had to look down.

'Good. You're the best friend I have.'

When I looked up, she had gone. We had both forgotten that my birthday party was at teatime on Friday. I had wanted to be at home with my mother when Ted's message had its effect.

Chapter 22 The Magic of the Deadly Nightshade

After my conversation with Marian I felt happy. She was kind and generous, and I loved her. But I did not agree with her actions. So I decided to have two separate opinions of her. But my happiness did not mean that the situation had improved. Our discussion of the secrets did not make them less dangerous.

What would happen if Marian told Ted not to be a soldier? Ted had said that she must make the decision. She had said that Ted was dangerous. If Marian asked him to, he might . . . That was the greatest danger. The end of the ninth Viscount might be the same as the end of the fifth.

Lord Trimingham's wishes were clear. He wanted to marry Marian. Marian wanted to marry Lord Trimingham, and she also wanted Ted to stay at Black Farm. What did Ted want? He had said that his own feelings were not important. I did not really believe that. He now knew that Marian was going to marry Lord Trimingham. And this had made him think about the army.

I was afraid for Lord Trimingham. I cried with Marian. But for Ted I felt very sorry. He was the only one who seemed to have a real life. I felt nearer to him than to the others. I was just their messenger, their go-between. But Ted felt that I had earned something. If Ted had asked me for advice, I would have told him to stay at Black Farm. He loved the place and his work there. If he went to the war, he might be killed. When I thought of Ted, he seemed too big to be killed.

I wondered whose fault it was. 'Nothing is ever a lady's fault,' Lord Trimingham had said. So Marian was not guilty. No one could say it was Lord Trimingham's fault. He had done nothing wrong. It must be Ted's fault. He had invited Marian into his kitchen, and he had put a spell on her. I now wanted to break that spell for everyone.

I had already begun to break it. Marian was not going to find him near the huts at six o'clock. Ted had said half past six. Was she prepared to wait half an hour for him? I did not think so. She did not like waiting for anything and usually did not wait more than five minutes. She might be angry with him. I imagined a fight between them.

Their love would end then, I hoped, and she would never see him again. The 'business' between Marian and Ted had ruined my holiday. It had ruined Marian's visit to London. It was pushing Ted away from the things he loved. It was making him join the army against his will. It filled our minds, and all our actions depended on it.

At that time I did not understand the power that attracted them to each other. It gave them something that I did not share. I was jealous of the thing that it gave them. Or jealous of the thing that they gave each other.

I decided to make a spell to break Ted's spell on Marian. My spell would have a better chance of success if it was a difficult one. I had to frighten myself while I was making it.

Marcus and I went to bed at our usual time. Half an hour later I put on some clothes and walked quietly down the stairs. I stopped outside the door of the main room. Inside, Marian was playing the piano, and someone was singing. The front door of the house was open. It was open every night in order to keep the house cool. But it was not cool.

I was frightened of the thing I had planned. The song ended, and I looked towards the darkness outside. I did not think that I was brave enough to go out there.

The voices inside were discussing the next song. I walked quietly to the door again and probably touched it with my foot. I heard Mrs Maudsley's voice.

'Denys, I think I heard a noise outside the door. Please see if anyone is there.'

Denys's steps came towards the door, and I ran outside. It was not completely dark, and I soon found the path.

My spell had to be made at night. I was sure that darkness would give it greater strength. I ran alone through the long grass. As I went, I thought about the details of my plan. Every part of the deadly nightshade was a strong poison. So the spell would have more effect if every part of the plant was used. I needed a leaf, flower and fruit to take back to my room.

In my room the necessary things were ready. They were:

A small bowl of oil (to heat the liquid)
One silver cup
One soap dish (with holes in it)
Four small books (to support the soap dish)
Four boxes of matches
Water
Watch (to measure the exact time)
Wet cloth (to guard against fire)

The success of my spell depended on the soap dish. I was going to place the cup in the soap dish so that the flames from the oil passed through the holes in the soap dish and heated the cup. My plan was to put a little water and pieces of the plant in the cup and boil it at twelve o'clock exactly. At the same time I intended to repeat the words of the spell thirteen times and then say, 'And I am thirteen, too.' Later, I was going to throw the liquid away in the bathroom. I had written all these details in my diary. Afterwards, I planned to pull the pages out, but I forgot to do that. The next day, Friday, I forgot many other things, too.

I reached the huts and saw the deadly nightshade. It was like a lady at the door of her house. 'Come in,' it seemed to say. I stretched out my hand and touched the flowers and leaves. They held my hand. If I went inside the hut, I would learn its secret, and it would learn mine. I went in. It was hot and soft and comfortable inside. A flower touched my face. Some of the fruit rubbed against my lips . . . When that happened, I was very frightened. I turned and tried to go out but I could not find the way. I was so frightened now that I began to break the plant. The plant was strong but I fought with it. Leaves, flowers and fruit fell to the ground around me. I held it tightly and pulled with all my strength. The plant tried to defend itself and then it gave up the fight. It came out of the ground, and I fell on my back outside. The deadly nightshade was destroyed.

Chapter 23 Birthday Morning

I slept very well that night. I did not wake up until a servant came into my room.

'Good morning, Henry!' I said.

'Good morning, sir,' he answered. 'I hope you will have a happy birthday.'

'Of course, it's my birthday!' I cried. 'I had forgotten it.'

'The others haven't forgotten,' he said.

Something in the room seemed different, and I looked at the window.

'Is it raining?' I asked.

'Not yet,' he replied. 'But I'm sure it will rain today. The ground needs some water. All this hot weather isn't natural.'

'Oh, but it's summer!' I complained.

'It isn't natural,' Henry repeated. 'Everything is burned brown. And a lot of people have gone crazy.'

'Gone crazy?' I said. 'Do you mean that the heat has made them go crazy?' I was very interested in craziness.

'Yes,' he said. 'It isn't only dogs that go crazy. People do, too.'

For a moment I thought about the strange relationship of Marian and Ted, and I wondered if that was caused by the heat.

As soon as Henry had gone, I thought about the previous night. Everything had been easy after my battle with the deadly nightshade. The front door was still open when I came back to the house. And I had been afraid of nothing.

Now the sky was grey. That was one reason why I felt strange. The sun seemed to have gone, and it was like losing a dear friend. I was so used to the heat that I hated this change. And there was another change. When I had destroyed the deadly nightshade, some of my old ideas had suffered, too. I seemed to understand, quite suddenly, that my spells were rather silly. It was my thirteenth birthday, and perhaps I was too old now to believe in spells and magic. I must learn how to control my imagination.

It had all started when Jenkins and Strode had fallen off the roof. But my spells had not *caused* the accident. I now believed that it could happen to anyone. And the fever at school was the same: the boys would have got it even if I had not written a spell. I was just playing at having some special power, and a lot of boys had believed it. I had also believed it myself, and that was even worse. I knew that my imagination was responsible for most of the trouble.

At Brandham I had imagined that I could control the weather. I thought I could stop the relationship between Marian and Ted. Marian had made me feel that she was depending on me. So my silly ideas were partly her fault. I felt ashamed of them now and ashamed, too, at trying to influence the events of life.

Perhaps the heat had made my brain soft, and a part of it had gone crazy. The heat and Marian had made Mrs Maudsley ill. Perhaps it was also the cause of Marcus's fever. But he had never lied to himself. He was interested in things that actually happened. He never tried to change them or to imagine other events. That was why he could not keep a secret. He preferred to tell the secret and then wait for something to happen. When I thought about these things, I admired Marcus very much.

What would he have said if he had seen my attack on the deadly nightshade? He would have thought that I was crazy. And everyone would have agreed. I was almost ready to agree myself.

Henry had put my green suit on a chair, but I decided not to wear it. The colour did not worry me at all now, but the suit made me think of my lies. So I put on my thick suit, socks and heavy boots.

At breakfast everyone talked about my birthday. Some of the guests made a few jokes about my suit but their words did not worry me. Two weeks ago the same jokes had made me cry!

Beside my plate there were two long envelopes. I recognized the writing. They were from my mother and my aunt. I usually read my letters in my room, but today I wanted all my actions to be public. So I asked everyone to excuse me, and I opened my mother's letter.

She seemed sorry that she had not sent me the telegram. She hoped that I was happy again. 'If you are still taking the messages,' she wrote, 'ask Mrs Maudsley to give them to a servant. I'm sure she will. I hope this small present will match your new suit.'

I looked into the envelope and took out a long, green tie.

'Oh, that *is* a beautiful tie!' said several people.

The other letter was longer because my aunt always wrote a lot about herself. She also liked to guess what I was doing, and her guesses were usually quite good ones.

'Your mother told me that you have a new suit,' she wrote. 'Green is an unusual colour for a boy's suit, perhaps, but I like it. People say that a woman can never choose a man's tie. But I think that's nonsense. I've chosen this one for you!'

It was another tie. The colour was almost yellow, and I did not like it very much. My friends did not seem to like it very much, and I guessed that Marcus was quite ready to criticize it. Suddenly Lord Trimingham stretched out his hand and said: 'Can I have a look at it, Leo?'

He took off his own blue and white tie and put on mine. 'I think it's very nice,' he said. 'It's the right kind of tie for watching the horses at Goodwood.'

I kept that tie for many years.

'Today is Leo's day,' Mrs Maudsley said, after breakfast. 'What would you like to do, Leo?'

I could not think of an answer, so Mrs Maudsley tried to help me.

'Shall we drive into the country and take lunch with us?'

'That sounds very nice,' I said.

'Or would you like to visit Beeston Castle after lunch? You haven't seen it, have you?'

'That would be very nice,' I repeated, not meaning it at all.

'So if it doesn't rain, we'll go to Beeston Castle,' she said. 'And at five o'clock you'll cut your birthday cake.'

'But Mother,' Denys said, 'we still don't know what *Leo* wants.'

'I think we do,' Mrs Maudsley said. 'You agree, Leo, don't you?'

'Oh, yes,' I said.

Mrs Maudsley turned to her older son. 'Are you satisfied, Denys?'

'We should let Leo choose on his birthday,' Denys said.

Mrs Maudsley's face showed no anger. 'Leo did not suggest anything,' she said, 'so–'

'I know, Mother, but on his *birthday*–'

'Can you suggest anything, Denys?' she asked.

'No, Mother, it isn't my birthday.'

Mrs Maudsley looked angry. 'That's enough,' she said. 'Leo has agreed to my suggestion.'

Outside, Marcus said to me: 'No, Leo, you can't wear that tie. Trimingham could wear it, of course. He can wear anything, but you have to dress with care.'

'Why?' I asked.

'You mustn't look common,' he replied. 'But I won't say any more because it's your birthday.'

During the morning I tried not to use my imagination. And I soon noticed that the morning was not very exciting. It was my birthday, but the day was not much different from any other day. I was afraid to visit the hut where I had killed the deadly nightshade. (I knew that a murderer likes to go back to the scene of his crime.) If I went there, I would certainly imagine all kinds of things.

I did not want to change my present opinion of spells. They were useless, even stupid, and I was too old to believe in them. But by lunchtime I knew that I could not look at my imagination in the same way. It was a part of my character. It gave me some of the pleasures that I most enjoyed. I felt uncomfortable in my thick suit, and I felt uncomfortable without my imagination. I almost hoped that Marcus would argue with me. When that idea entered my mind, I had to change my plan. I knew that I would never be happy without my own private thoughts.

I went to my room then and put on my green suit. After that I felt a lot better.

Chapter 24 Storms at Brandham Hall

After lunch the sky was dark with clouds, and we all expected thunder. Mrs Maudsley decided to wait for a quarter of an hour. If then it still looked like thunder, we would not go to Beeston Castle.

We were all standing near the front door. Marian said, 'Come with me, Leo, and tell me about the weather.'

I followed her outside and looked up at the sky. 'I think–' I began.

'You needn't,' she said. 'If we don't go to Beeston, would you like a walk?'

'Oh, yes,' I said immediately. 'Will you come with me?'

'I'd like to,' she answered, 'but it's not that kind of walk. It's this.' As she was speaking her hand touched mine. She gave me a letter.

'Oh no!' I cried. I felt disappointed and angry.

'But I say "Yes".' She was not annoyed with me this time, but she began to laugh loudly. She was laughing, I thought, to hide my surprise and disappointment from the others. I started arguing with her. That made her laugh more, and then, giving up, I laughed too. We probably made a lot of noise.

'Marian! Leo!'

It was Mrs Maudsley's voice. She walked slowly down the steps. Marian was still laughing, but I had stopped.

'What are you arguing about?' Mrs Maudsley asked.

'Oh, I was teaching him to be polite,' Marian said. She did not say any more because at that moment I dropped the letter. It lay on the ground between us.

'Were you arguing about that letter?' Mrs Maudsley asked.

Marian picked it up and pushed it into my pocket.

'Yes, Mother,' she said. 'I asked Leo to take it to Nannie Robson. I'd like to visit her this afternoon. But Leo refused to take it! He pretended that he and Marcus were busy.'

'It needn't worry you, Marian,' Mrs Maudsley said. She looked directly at Marian and then at me. 'You say that she never remembers your visits. I thought that Leo and I might have a walk in the garden. It isn't fine enough to go to Beeston this afternoon. Come, Leo. You haven't yet seen all of the garden. Marcus doesn't like flowers very much.'

I had an idea that I needed some protection from Mrs Maudsley, so I said, 'Would you like Marcus to come with us?'

'Oh, no,' she said. 'You've been playing with him all morning. He's very fond of you, Leo, and Marian is, too. We all are.'

This speech made me happy but I did not know the right answer.

'You have all been very kind to me,' I said.

'Have we? I thought perhaps we had not given you enough attention. First Marcus was ill, and then I was in bed for a few days. I hope the others looked after you.'

'Oh, yes, they did,' I said.

We had reached the garden.

'Are you interested in flowers?' she asked.

I said that I was very interested in dangerous flowers.

She smiled. 'There aren't many of that kind here.'

I told her about the deadly nightshade.

'It was in one of those old huts,' I said, 'behind the house.'

I stopped then. I did not want to go on.

Marcus and I had heard the voices near those huts. I wondered

'Were you arguing about that letter?'

if he had told his mother about them.

We stopped beside a big pink flower, and Mrs Maudsley said: 'This always makes me think of Marian. Do you often carry messages for her?'

I thought as quickly as I could.

'No, not often,' I said. 'Just once or twice.'

'I'm worried because of that note to Nannie Robson. Would you like to go now? You know the way, of course.'

This was an opportunity. I could escape if I wanted to. But what would I say to her?

'I'd like to go. I'm not quite sure of the way, but I can ask someone.'

'Ask someone?' she repeated. 'But haven't you taken messages there before?'

'Oh, yes. Yes, I have.'

'Why aren't you sure of the way then?'

I did not answer.

'Listen,' she said. 'Someone should deliver that note. I'll call one of the servants and ask him to take it.'

My skin suddenly felt cold. 'Oh no, Mrs Maudsley,' I said. 'It isn't very important.'

'It's important to Nannie Robson,' Mrs Maudsley said. 'Old people like to prepare something for a visitor.'

Then she called one of the men who were working there. He stopped work and came towards us. I put my hand in my pocket.

'Stanton,' Mrs Maudsley said, 'we have a rather urgent note for Miss Robson. Would you mind taking it?'

Stanton agreed and held out his hand.

My fingers moved in my pocket. I felt in several of them and then said: 'I haven't got it! I'm very sorry. Perhaps it fell out somewhere.'

'Feel again,' Mrs Maudsley said. 'Feel again.'

I felt in all my pockets but did not take out the note.

Mrs Maudsley said, 'Stanton, just tell Miss Robson that Miss Marian will visit her this afternoon.'

I wanted to follow Stanton when he left us. But I could not do that. Mrs Maudsley was looking at me carefully.

'I could search your pockets,' she said, 'but I won't do that. You said that you have taken messages for Marian before. I want to ask you one question. If you don't take them to Nannie Robson, who do you take them to?'

I could not answer. But an answer came from the sky. There was a crash of thunder. Rain began immediately. We ran to the house. And when we reached it, I went straight to my room. There, I received another shock. All my things had gone. Some other guest had moved into the room. I stayed in the bathroom until teatime. Everything was ready for my birthday tea. The cake was in the middle of the table.

'Sit beside me, please, Leo,' Mrs Maudsley said.

I walked slowly to that uncomfortable place, but I did not have to worry. Her attitude had changed.

'I'm sorry about your room,' she said. 'We needed it for another guest. Your things are in Marcus's room. Are you pleased to share with him again?'

'Yes, of course,' I said.

'Marian wants to give you her present first,' she said. 'Can you wait?'

'When is she coming?'

'About six o'clock, we think. She won't stay very long with Nannie Robson.'

She smiled, but I noticed that her hands were shaking.

'Did you get wet?' I asked. I had to say something about our talk. I could not believe that she had forgotten it.

'Not very wet.' She laughed. 'But if you'd been a gentleman, you'd have waited for me.'

'But he is a gentleman,' Lord Trimingham said. 'He's quite a lady-killer. Marian has great confidence in him.'

Mrs Maudsley changed the subject. She said, 'It's time that Leo cut the cake.'

Someone put the cake in front of me. I cut a few pieces.

Lord Trimingham looked at his watch.

'Marian should be here now,' he said.

'It's still raining,' Mr Maudsley said. 'We'd better send a driver to Nannie Robson's house. Why didn't we think of that before?' He rang the bell and gave the order.

We ate the cake, but left one thick piece on the plate for Marian.

'She'll be here in ten minutes,' Lord Trimingham said.

'Perhaps she didn't wait,' someone said. 'She may be on foot in the rain. She'll be so wet that she'll have to change her clothes.'

Mrs Maudsley gave everyone another cup of tea, and there was a pause in the conversation. For the last fifteen minutes there had been a pause after every movement and almost every speech. At one time everybody seemed to be talking. And it was then that I heard the sound of the horses outside. A few minutes later a servant came into the room and spoke to Mrs Maudsley.

'Excuse me,' he said. 'The driver has come back but not Miss Marian. She wasn't at Miss Robson's. Miss Robson said that she hadn't seen her today.'

Although I had been expecting this news, it still gave me a shock.

'Where *can* she be?' someone asked.

'She may be in her room,' Denys said. 'Perhaps she's changing her clothes.'

'We shall just have to wait for her,' Mr Maudsley said, calmly.

But Mrs Maudsley pushed her chair back and stood up. Her body was bent and shaking. Her face had changed and was unrecognizable.

'No,' she said. 'We won't wait. I'm going to look for her. Leo, you know where she is. You can show me the way.'

I did not really know what was happening. She caught my hand and pulled me behind her. 'Madeleine!' her husband cried. It was the only time that I ever heard her name.

Outside the room I saw the green bicycle, and I have never forgotten that first quick look at it. It was resting against the stairs and shining as brightly as silver.

Then we were outside in the rain. I did not know that Mrs Maudsley could run fast. She ran so fast now that it was difficult to stay beside her. We were soon very wet, but I was too frightened to worry about the rain.

Mrs Maudsley said nothing. She ran with wide, long steps, and her skirt was moving through the wet earth. It was soon clear that she was guiding me. When we came to the path between the trees, I tried to stop her.

I cried, 'Not this way, Mrs Maudsley!'

She did not listen to me but hurried forward. Then we reached the hut where I had killed the deadly nightshade. The broken branches were still lying on the path. She stopped and looked inside the hut.

'Not here,' she said, moving away, 'but here, perhaps . . . or here.'

There was no sound from the row of huts. I did not want to search with her, and I tried to free my hand from hers. I began to cry.

'No,' she said, 'you *must* come with me.' And she pulled me forward.

And then we saw them. They were lying together on the ground. Marian and Ted Burgess. I did not understand. But I guessed that they were spooning. Mrs Maudsley's loud cries frightened me. They were louder than any cries that I had ever heard.

I remember very little more. I must have been ill, because I stayed in bed for two or three days. But before I left Brandham Hall, I heard and understood one thing: Ted Burgess had gone home that evening and shot himself.

Chapter 25 The End of the Story

My illness lasted about six weeks, and I do not remember very much about it. Clearly someone brought me home to West Hatch. The doctor and my mother tried to make me remember the last events at Brandham. But I would not have said anything even if I had been able to remember.

'You haven't done anything *bad*, Leo,' my mother used to say. 'You needn't feel ashamed. It's finished now.'

But I did not believe her. I felt ashamed of many things. I thought that I had made them all suffer – Lord Trimingham, Ted, Marian and all the Maudsley family. I did not know, and did not want to know, the results of my behaviour.

For Ted Burgess the result was death. That was partly why my experience at Brandham was not 'finished'. In my mind there were the most terrible pictures of Ted's dead body.

I did not think that the people at Brandham had behaved badly. I had succeeded in the cricket match and at the concert, but in the third test I had failed. When Mrs Maudsley had discovered Marian and Ted together on the ground, she had defeated me. And now I was vanquished for ever.

At school my spells had brought me success, and at Brandham, too, my last spell had been a success. At least, it had stopped the relationship between Ted and Marian. It had also destroyed the deadly nightshade. But then, like some dangerous pet, it had turned against its controller. It had destroyed Ted and perhaps destroyed me.

I had come into Ted's life by chance. A strange boy from some distant place had appeared and played in the haystack at Black Farm. From that moment, I now believed, Ted's end was certain. And mine was certain too, because our lives were joined together and I could not hurt him without hurting myself.

At school I had used my magic power to influence ordinary people and ordinary events. At Brandham I had tried to use it against people who were *not* ordinary. And that was why it had failed. I had tried to make the gods fight one another!

My experience at Brandham seemed to kill my belief in other people and most of my love for them. It also proved that my imagination was of no use to me. From then until now I have lived mainly without friends. I have enjoyed little love and little of the happiness that love brings. I have managed to live without the great pleasure that my imagination used to give me.

When Marcus and I met again at school, we were polite but not friends. No one noticed this because the other boys there often changed their friends. As time passed, I became less and less interested in people in almost every way. Another pleasure helped me, the pleasure that I had always had from facts. I began to collect facts, and I soon recognized that they were really valuable. They were independent of me, and my private desires could not change them. I thought they were the only true things in the world. They probably saved my life too. The Great War started in 1914. I was twenty-seven then, but I did not have to join the army. The government thought that my skill with facts was more important work.

My mother had kept all the letters that I had written to her. They were not in the red box where I had found the diary, but I soon discovered them and decided to read them again. They might help, I thought, to explain some of the problems of my Brandham experience.

One thing became clear immediately. Marian had been quite

fond of me *before* the messages started. She had later told me a lot of lies, but the green suit came first. I understood now the main reason for our visit to Norwich: she wanted to meet Ted Burgess. But she was also worried about the heat and my thick suit.

It was certain, too, that Marcus always told his mother everything. He had made me so angry once that I had talked about Marian. I claimed to know where she went in the evenings and he probably repeated the claim to his mother. At school Marcus knew how to keep a secret, but at home he behaved differently. I did not know then that people's habits changed with their situations.

For several months after my visit to Brandham, I believed that everything that had happened there was my fault. I thought that I had been wrong to read Marian's note to Ted. I was wrong to change the time in Ted's last message to her. If I had told her 'half past six', my birthday party would have been a great success. Mrs Maudsley would not then have gone out to look for Marian. My intention had been good, but the result had been terrible. Since that time I have never taken an interest, for good or bad, in other people's business.

When, later, I considered my spells, especially the last one, I had to shake my head. They were nothing, of course. They did not agree at all with the world of facts. In time it was the search for facts that calmed my mind.

My memory and my diary gave me enough facts for this story. But the facts did not satisfy me. Like the plates on the wall of Brandham Church, they were not complete. They did not tell me if my decisions were sensible. They told me nothing about happiness or unhappiness. I needed other facts with which I could compare my own. And I would have to get them from *other* people – the other people in the story.

But at that moment my thoughts were interrupted. I discovered a letter. I remembered it immediately. It was Marian's last note to Ted. My mother probably found it in my pocket when I came home. Mrs Maudsley had almost found it, too. If she *had* found it, everything would have been different! But I was interested only in facts, and the note might contain a new one. I opened the envelope and read:

Dearest,

I expect our messenger made a mistake. You can't mean six o'clock. At that time there'll be hay in your hair and dust on your clothes! I can't meet you in that condition. So come at half past six if you can. It's our dear messenger's birthday, and I must be there to give him a present. It's exactly the right present for a messenger. He won't have to walk to the farm in future! If he doesn't deliver it, I shall be there at six. And I'll wait until seven or eight or nine – dearest, dearest.

Tears came into my eyes. They were my first tears for more than fifty years. She had given me the bicycle for my journeys to the farm! I was sorry now that I had not kept it. After my illness I had told my mother to give it away. I had never ridden it.

I decided to go back to Brandham. I stayed at the hotel in Norwich where Marian and I had had lunch. The next day I hired a car and drove to the village.

The place had changed of course and, after fifty years, I did not recognize it. I wondered where I might find the least change. And I knew that that would be the church. I went there immediately.

There were two new plates on the wall.

'Hugh Winlove, ninth Viscount Trimingham,' I read. 'Born 15th November 1874, died 6th July 1910.'

Poor Hugh! He had lived for only ten years after my visit. I wondered if he had ever married. The plate did not say anything about a Viscountess, but I turned to the other new one. It was far from the others in the corner of the wall.

'Hugh Maudsley Winlove, tenth Viscount Trimingham. Born 12th February 1901, killed in the Battle of Normandy, 15th June 1944. And Alethea, his wife, killed in an air attack on London, 16th January 1941.'

If these were facts, then I did not understand them. Lord Trimingham was not married when I left Brandham Hall. But this plate showed that he had had a son six or seven months later.

I know now why I did not understand. I had always thought that Marian was dead. In my thoughts she had died immediately after that last terrible scene at the huts. I did not think that she could ever go on living. And even after fifty years that idea was still stuck in my mind.

I left the church and walked down the main street of the village. My plan was a simple one. I hoped to find the oldest person there. He or she would be able to tell me the necessary facts. Then I saw a man whose face seemed less unfamiliar than the others. He was about twenty-five years old and not the kind of person I was looking for. But there was one question that he might be able to answer.

'Excuse me,' I said, 'but is there still a Lord Trimingham at Brandham Hall?'

At first I thought that he did not want to answer. He seemed annoyed that I had interrupted his thoughts.

He said, 'There is, and in fact I am Lord Trimingham.'

I was very surprised and looked hard at his face. It was the colour of his skin that made me think of something. It was a golden colour.

'You seem surprised,' he said. 'I live only in a corner of the house. The rest of it has become a school for girls.'

'I'm sorry,' I said. 'But I'm glad you live there. I stayed there many years ago.'

His attitude changed immediately, and he said, with interest: 'When did you stay there?'

'It was when your grandfather was alive,' I said.

'My grandfather?' he said. He seemed anxious about something. 'Did you know my grandfather?'

'Yes,' I said, 'the ninth Viscount. He was your grandfather, wasn't he?'

'Of course,' Lord Trimingham said, 'I never knew him, I'm afraid. He died before I was born. But I believe he was a very nice man.'

I smiled. 'He was,' I agreed.

'And did you also know my grandmother?'

I was surprised once again, and wanted time to think.

'Your grandmother?' I said.

'Yes, she was a Miss Maudsley,' he said.

I took a long breath. 'Oh yes,' I said. 'I knew her very well. Is she still alive?'

'She is,' he said, but there was not much happiness in his voice.

'And where does she live?'

'Here, in the village. She lives in a little house that used to belong to Miss Robson. Did you know her, too?'

'No,' I said. 'I never saw her, but I heard about her. Is your grandmother well?'

'Quite well,' he said, 'but she forgets things rather easily. Many old people do, of course.' He smiled then, and went on: 'Why don't you go and see her? She's rather lonely. She doesn't have many visitors.'

The past seemed to take control of my voice. 'I'd better not,' I said. 'She may not want to see me.'

He was confused, I knew. He said, 'You must decide about that.'

He was a much younger man than I. And that, I thought, might give me a claim to his help. I decided to speak freely.

'Will you be kind enough to help me?' I asked.

'Of course. But how?'

'Will you tell Lady Trimingham that Leo Colston is here. Say that I would like to see her.'

He thought for a moment. 'I don't usually go to her house,' he said. 'I telephone sometimes. Was there a telephone here when you came before?'

'No,' I replied. 'It would have helped a lot if there had been.'

'Yes, it would,' he said. 'My grandmother talks a lot. But I'll go if you like. I . . .' He stopped then.

'I'd be very glad if you did,' I said. 'I don't want to – to surprise her.' I thought of the last time I had done so.

'I'll go,' he said. 'It's Mr Leo Colston, isn't it? Do you think she'll remember the name?'

'I'm sure she will,' I said. 'I'll wait here for you.'

While I was waiting I walked about the street, but I saw nothing that I could remember. Then I saw the young man and went to meet him. His face looked worried, and it looked very like Ted Burgess's face.

'She didn't remember you at first,' he said. 'And then she remembered you very well. She said she would be very pleased to see you. She was worried about lunch. She asked me to give it to you because she can't. Would you like that?'

'Yes,' I replied, 'if it's no trouble.'

'I would be happy if you came,' he said, but he did not look at all happy. 'Grandmother wasn't sure that you'd want to come to the Hall.'

'Oh, why?' I asked.

'Because of something that happened long ago. You were only a little boy, she said. And she said it wasn't her fault.'

'Your grandfather used to say that nothing is ever a lady's fault,' I said.

He looked very hard at me.

'Yes,' I said, 'I knew your grandfather very well, and you are very like him.'

He changed colour. And I noticed that he was standing away from me. His real grandfather had stood just like that when we last met.

His face was red now. 'I'm very sorry,' he said, 'if we didn't behave well towards you.'

I liked his saying 'we', and I remembered how sorry Ted had been about many things. I said quickly: 'Oh, it happened long, long ago. Please don't think about it. Your grandmother . . . Do you often see her?'

'Not very often.'

'And not many people visit her. Is that right?'

'Not very many,' he said.

'Then why does she go on living in the village?'

'I just don't know,' he said.

'She was very beautiful.'

'I've often heard that,' he said. 'But I don't quite see it. Do you know the way to the house?'

'No, but I can ask someone.' I remembered that I had given the same answer once before. To Mrs Maudsley.

He did not offer to go with me, but he showed me the way. Then he added: 'We'll have lunch about one o'clock.' And I promised to be there. He walked away, but after a moment he turned. He came back and then stopped. Without looking at me, he said: 'Were you the little boy who . . . ?'

'Yes,' I said.

◆

Marian was sitting in front of a window. When I entered the room, a young servant said, 'Mr Colston.' Marian got up and held out her hand uncertainly.

'Is this really–?' she began.

Marian got up and held out her hand uncertainly.

'I recognize you,' I said. 'But I didn't expect you would know me.'

Actually, if I had seen her in the street, I would not have recognized her. Only her eyes had kept their quality, although they were less bright.

We talked a little about my journey, and I told her something of my work. Then I said, 'My life has not really been a very exciting one.'

She said, 'You lost your memory at the beginning of your life. I'm losing mine at the end. Sometimes I'm not quite sure what happened yesterday. But I remember the past very clearly.'

I asked her several questions then, and she said: 'Marcus was killed in the first war, and Denys, too. I think Denys was killed first. Marcus was your friend, wasn't he? Yes, of course he was. He was Mother's favourite, and mine too.'

'What happened to your mother?' I asked.

'Poor Mother! It was very sad. But I was soon well again. We didn't have the dance, of course. Your mother came here, and I remember her well. She was a sweet woman, with grey eyes, like yours, and brown hair. You didn't speak to anyone for two or three days, and Mother couldn't stop crying. You stayed until Monday, I remember. We never found out how you had heard about Ted. Perhaps Henry told you. Wasn't he one of your friends?'

'How did you know that I had heard?'

'Because you said, "Why did Ted shoot himself? I thought he could shoot straight." You probably thought it was an accident. But it wasn't, of course. Ted had a weak spot in his character, like Edward.'

'Edward?'

'My grandson. Ted didn't need to kill himself. People soon forget that kind of thing.'

'And Hugh?' I asked.

'He married me. He didn't worry about it. Hugh was true to me. He refused to listen to a word of criticism. If people didn't want to know us, we didn't think about them. But we had lots of friends. I was Lady Trimingham, of course. I still am. There isn't another.'

'What was your son's wife like?' I asked.

'Poor Alethea? Oh, she was a very unhappy girl. And her parties were so sad that I rarely went to them. But people came to me, of course – interesting people, like artists and writers. My son wasn't fond of living in the country. He was like my father, but he hadn't Father's strong character. Father was a wonderful man, and Mother was wonderful, too. I was lucky to have parents like them.'

'You haven't told me about your mother,' I noted.

'Poor Mother! She couldn't stay with us, of course. She had to go to hospital, but we often went to see her. She was glad that I married Hugh.'

'And your father?'

'Oh, Father lived until he was nearly ninety. He often came to see us at the Hall, and he visited me for many years after Hugh died. We were all very fond of one another.'

I did not want to hear much more, but the facts were not yet complete.

'Aren't you lonely here?' I asked. 'Why don't you move to London?'

'Lonely?' she said. 'What do you mean? Lots of people come to see me. They all know about me. They want to see me just as you did.'

'I'm very glad I came. And I was pleased to meet your grandson, Edward.'

'You mustn't call him Edward,' she said. 'It's a family name, of course, but he prefers Hugh.'

'You must be very glad that he's near you,' I said.

Her face changed then. I thought that she was going to cry.

'I am,' she said. Then she corrected herself: 'I would be if he came to see me. He doesn't come often.'

'Doesn't he?' I said.

'No. Hundreds of other people come, but he doesn't. Do you remember how often I used to visit old Nannie Robson?'

Before I could say anything, she asked: 'Does he make you think of anyone?'

I was surprised that she asked me that question. 'Yes, he does,' I said. 'His grandfather.'

'That's right, that's right. And he knows, of course. He thinks it's my fault. He's the only person in the world who thinks that. I'm his own grandmother! People have told me that he wants to get married. *He* has never told me. She's a nice girl, but he won't ask her because he's afraid. He thinks he's under some kind of spell, and he's afraid that he'll pass it on to his children. It's all very stupid. But you can help, Leo, if you will.'

'I?'

'Yes, you. You know the facts. You know what *really* happened. And except for me, only *you* know. Edward mustn't believe the silly stories that he has heard. You know that Ted and I were in love. But it wasn't the ordinary kind of love. It was a very beautiful thing. It was something that anyone might be proud of. Don't you agree, Leo?'

I could not say anything except 'Yes'.

'I'm glad you agree because you made us happy. And we made you happy, didn't we? You were only a little boy, but we shared our great happiness with you. If we hadn't shown it to you, perhaps you would never have known anything about love. But Edward–' She stopped. 'But you can tell him, Leo. Tell him everything, just as it happened. He needn't feel ashamed of it, and he needn't feel ashamed of me. It was a beautiful thing. It wasn't bad or ugly, was it? And it didn't hurt anyone at all. We had some terrible times, of course. Hugh died, and then Marcus and Denys were killed. Then, in the second war, my son Hugh was killed, and his wife. But that was the fault of this terrible century in which death and hate have driven away life and love. Go to Edward, Leo, and tell him this. You used to love taking our messages, didn't you? And this is another message of love. He has this silly idea that he can't marry. It hurts me more than anything else. I think every man should get married. But Edward is young. He's the same age as Ted was in 1900. Tell him he must forget his stupid ideas. His grandfather had stupid ideas too. Poor Ted, if he had had more brains, he wouldn't have blown them out. You must do this for us, Leo. Tell Edward there's no spell except hate in the heart.'

I felt very glad when she stopped. We talked a little more, and then I stood up. I promised to visit her again.

'Thank you!' she cried. 'You're the best friend I have. Kiss me, Leo!' Her face was wet with tears.

I went out into the street. I was surprised at the way she had lied to herself completely for more than fifty years. I could not understand why her words had had a powerful effect on me. And I was almost sorry that I could not lie to myself in the same way.

I had not promised to give Edward her message of love. I was not a child who she could give orders to. My car was standing by the post office. I could easily telephone Ted's grandson and make an excuse.

But I did not. I drove to Brandham Hall. And on the way I wondered how I should give him the message. Soon I saw the house through the trees.

ACTIVITIES

Chapters 1–5

Before you read

1 The writer, L.P. Hartley, was very interested in the society and customs of his time. What do you know, or what can you imagine, about the social classes in England in 1900? How were they different from each other? Did they mix with each other?

2 The main character in *The Go-Between* is Leo, a boy who will soon be thirteen years old, and we see the story through his eyes. Do you know any other books or films with a young boy or girl at the centre of the story? Does the young person change during the story? Does he or she learn anything important about adult life?

3 Look at the Word List at the back of this book. Answer the questions.

   a What should you do if a child eats some *deadly nightshade?*

   b How do people feel when they are *defeated* or *vanquished*?

   c Name three illnesses for which a doctor or nurse might use a *thermometer*.

   d In what countries is *cricket* a popular sport? Can you explain how to keep *score* in a *cricket* match?

   e Who do you expect to use magic *spells*? Do you think magic *spells* work?

   f People *clap* if they enjoy a good performance. What other ways can people show that they like something?

   g What modern types of communication have made *telegrams* old-fashioned?

   h How would you describe a person that you would call an *angel*?

While you read

4 Who is it? Write the correct name.

a .... writes magic spells in a diary.
b .... is always on the winning side at school.
c .... invites Leo Colston to Brandham Hall.
d .... has an older brother and sister.
e .... only looks at people for a purpose.
f .... is tall and beautiful.
g .... feels poor and common.
h .... is called Hugh.
i .... buys his ties at Challow and Crawshay's.
j .... lies about the trip to Norwich with Leo.
k .... has plans for Marian's future.
l .... speaks with the local accent.
m .... has a strong, perfect body.
n .... complains about wet hair.
o .... feels happy after helping Marian.

After you read

5 Are these statements true or false? Correct the false ones.

a The storyteller, Leo Colston, is a married man who lives with his wife and children.
b The beginning of the twentieth century is exciting for Leo.
c Jenkins and Strode are Leo's best friends at school.
d Leo's parents are very different from each other.
e Leo is well-known at school for his magic spells.
f Leo packs summer clothes for his trip to Brandham Hall in July.
g Mr Maudsley is the boss at Brandham Hall.
h Marcus tells his mother secrets.
i Leo thinks that the deadly nightshade plant is attractive.
j The weather causes problems for Leo.
k Marian laughs at Leo's heavy clothes and makes him cry.
l Marian and her mother always agree with each other.
m Leo's trip to Norwich with Marian is a great success.
n Marcus describes Trimingham as a very handsome man.
o Something about the visit to the river excites Marian.

6 What is happening in each of these situations? How are the people probably feeling?
   a 'On the last evening my mother and I sat together in silence.'
   b 'I knew that everyone was laughing at me, and I hated it.'
   c 'She let me touch her hair. It was dry with the dryness that I had given her.'

Chapters 6–10

Before you read

7 The shopping trip to Norwich to buy clothes is important to Leo and Marian for different reasons. Why do people sometimes understand situations differently?

8 Deadly nightshade is both beautiful and dangerous. Can you think of any people or situations that can be described in this way?

While you read

9 Does Leo feel good (✓) or bad (✗) about these?
   a telling bad news .....
   b news of a dance .....
   c walking to church with Marian .....
   d being in church for a long time .....
   e not being told that Trimingham is the ninth viscount .....
   f hot weather .....
   g the silence near the swimming place .....
   h jumping from the top of the haystack .....
   i Ted Burgess's house .....
   j Marian washing his knee .....
   k Lord Trimingham naming him Mercury .....
   l a letter from his mother .....
   m carrying notes between Marian and Ted Burgess .....
   n the possibility that Ted Burgess is in trouble with the police .....
   o telling Marcus lies .....

After you read

10 Put these events in the correct order.

- **a** Leo reads part of a letter from Marian to Ted Burgess.
- **b** Leo is introduced to Hugh Trimingham.
- **c** Marian cleans Leo's leg.
- **d** Leo agrees to carry a message from Ted to Marian.
- **e** Leo is asked to look for Marian.
- **f** There is a meal in the country.
- **g** Leo and the family go to church.
- **h** Leo carries a message about a book.
- **i** Marcus feels better and gets up.
- **j** Leo hurts his leg.
- **k** Marcus becomes ill.
- **l** Leo meets Ted Burgess at the farm.

11 Leo has carried three messages to Marian.

- **a** In what ways are Lord Trimingham's messages different from Ted Burgess's?
- **b** How does Marian feel in each case?
- **c** Why is Leo upset about the letter with the open envelope?

12 Work with another student. Act out the first conversation between Leo and Ted, from the moment when Leo cuts his knee. Discuss who you are, Leo's knee, the green suit and carrying the letter.

Chapters 11–15

Before you read

13 Leo likes to check the thermometer every day, always hoping for higher temperatures. In your opinion, how can the weather affect how people behave?

14 Cricket is a popular summer game. What outdoor games are popular in your country? Why do people enjoy them?

While you read

15 Circle the correct word in each statement.

a Leo feels *proud/ ashamed* that he knows Marian and Ted Burgess's secret.

b Ted reminds Leo that Marian is *special/ unimportant* to both of them.

c Spooning is a *mysterious/ dull* subject for Leo.

d *Eleven/ twelve* men play on each team in a cricket match.

e Both Marian and Trimingham seem *disappointed/ pleased* by the messages about the concert.

f The two cricket teams show how *similar/ different* the social classes are.

g Mr Maudsley's *intelligence/ strength* makes him a good cricketer.

h Marian becomes very *bored/ excited* when Ted begins to score.

i Leo is *certain/ uncertain* about his feelings after catching Ted's ball.

j It is *difficult/ easy* for Ted to smile at Marian after he sings a romantic song.

k Marcus *discusses/ doesn't discuss* private subjects with his mother.

l The death of the fifth Viscount Trimingham was caused by *war/ jealousy*.

After you read

16 Who is speaking, who are they talking to, and what are they talking about?

a 'If you spoon with someone, will that person have a baby?'

b 'Oh, no. Do you want me to go home?'

c 'He's an excellent messenger.'

d 'Although he was the smallest man on the field, he defeated one of the greatest.'

e 'Everyone will be told at the dance.'

17 Imagine you are Leo. Explain what you did and how you felt from the moment of Pollin's accident during the match.

or

Imagine you are Lord Trimingham. Explain how you felt during the concert.

18 Discuss these words from Lord Trimingham: 'Nothing is ever a lady's fault.'

a Do you agree? Why/why not?

b What do these words tell us about relations between men and women at that time and in that social class?

Chapters 16–20

Before you read

19 Marcus describes Leo as 'green', which means that he does not have much experience and does not understand adult life. Does 'green' mean this in your language? Do other colours have a special meaning?

While you read

20 What does Leo do next? Look at the sentences below these and write the numbers 1–9.

a Leo hears about Marcus's plan to visit Nannie Robson. .....

b Leo realises that Marian is still in love with Ted Burgess. .....

c Marian offers to pay Leo for carrying her messages. .....

d Leo understands that Marian doesn't love him. .....

e Ted Burgess offers to give Leo something for being a messenger. .....

f Leo runs from Black Farm and returns to his room at the Hall. .....

g Leo goes with Marcus to the hut where the deadly nightshade grows. .....

h Leo receives a letter from Ted. .....

i Leo says goodbye to Ted. .....

1) He offers to deliver one more message for Ted.

2) He cries and cries.

3) He talks to Trimingham in the smoking room.

4) He goes to check the temperature.

5) He asks for the facts about spooning.

6) He takes Marian's letter and runs away.

7) He hears Marian's and Ted's voices.

8) He worries that someone will die.

9) He writes a letter to his mother.

After you read

21 Explain why these people get angry or annoyed with Leo.

a Marian, when she finds Leo at the thermometer.

b Ted Burgess, when Leo is in his kitchen.

c Lord Trimingham, when Leo is going to post a letter to his mother.

22 Explain why Leo gets angry with Marcus in these situations.

a When they are walking towards the huts.

b When they are talking about the dance.

23 Work with another student. Act out the conversation that you think Lord Trimingham has with Ted Burgess about the army.

Chapters 21–25

Before you read

24 What do you think will happen to these people by the end of the story?

a Marian **b** Ted **c** Lord Trimingham **d** Leo

While you read

25 How do these people die?

a Ted Burgess ....

b Hugh, tenth Viscount Trimingham ....

c Alethea Winlove ....

d Marcus and Denys Maudsley ....

e old Mr Maudsley ....

After you read

26 On which day – Wednesday, Thursday or Friday – did these events happen?

a Leo receives two ties.
b Marian learns that Hugh has talked to Ted about becoming a soldier.
c Ted Burgess shoots himself.
d Leo destroys the deadly nightshade.
e Mrs Maudsley appears at breakfast and is kind to Leo.
f There's a letter on the tea table for Leo.
g Marian and Leo both lie to Mrs Maudsley.
h There's a change in the weather.
i Mrs Maudsley sees that Marian has given Leo a letter to deliver.
j Marian kisses Leo.

27 Discuss why these things or people are important to the story.

a the letter to Leo from his mother
b Lord Trimingham's powerful position in society
c the deadly nightshade
d Mrs Maudsley's illness
e a yellow tie for Leo's birthday
f Nannie Robson
g thunder and rain
h spells

28 Work with another student. Act out a conversation between Leo Colston and Edward, the eleventh Viscount Trimingham, after Leo has visited Marian.

a Leo tells the young man the story of his visit to Brandham Hall in 1900 as he remembers it.
or
b Leo tells the story as Marian remembers it.

Writing

29 Imagine that you are Marcus and want your mother to invite Leo to stay at Brandham Hall. Write a letter to your mother, with a description of Leo.

30 Compare the backgrounds and characters of Ted Burgess and Lord Trimingham.

31 Describe how Leo's character changes after his birthday.

32 'You haven't done anything *bad*, Leo,' my mother used to say. 'You needn't feel ashamed.' Do you agree with Leo's mother, or do you think Leo should be ashamed of his behaviour?

33 You are the ninth Lord Trimingham in June 1910. You are ill and know you are going to die soon. Write a letter to your nine-year-old son about love and duty.

34 As an old lady, Marian tells Leo that her love for Ted 'didn't hurt anyone at all'. How true do you think this is?

35 When Leo visits Marian in the 1950s, she tells him that her mother 'had to go to hospital'. Write the doctor's report explaining Mrs Maudsley's 'illness'.

36 Imagine that you are Leo Colston. Write a page in your diary about your visit to Brandham Hall after more than fifty years.

37 Which adult character in the story do you like most? Why?

38 It is 1953 and *The Go-Between* has just appeared. Write a report on this new book for your local newspaper. Would you suggest that people read it? Why (not)?

WORD LIST

angel (n) a messenger and servant of God, usually with wings and dressed in white, believed to live in Heaven

audience (n) the people who listen to or watch a performance

battle (n) a fight between two armies; a fight for power

claim (n/v) a statement that something is true although it has not been proved, or that something belongs to you

clap (v) to hit your hands together repeatedly to show that you enjoyed something

cricket (n) a game played outside by two teams; players win points by hitting the ball and then running

darling (adj) much loved

deadly nightshade (n) a poisonous plant

defeat (n/v) the state of being beaten in a fight or competition; if you defeat someone, you win

depend on (v) to know that someone will help you when you need help; if something depends on something else, it will only happen in that situation

disappoint (v) to make someone unhappy because they hoped for something that did not happen

hay (n) grass that has been cut and dried; a **haystack** is a pile of hay

headmaster (n) the male teacher who is in charge of a school

hesitate (v) to pause for a moment before doing or saying something

influence (n) the power to affect what someone does or what happens

lion (n) a large, wild member of the cat family which is found in Africa

nonsense (n) a statement which is stupid or untrue

priest (n) someone who performs religious duties, for example in the Catholic church

regret (v) to feel sorry about something you have done or something that has happened

row (n) a line of things next to each other

rub (v) to move across something while pressing on it

score (n/v) the number of points won in a game

sore (adj) painful because you have hurt yourself or you are ill

spell (n) special words used to make magic happen

surface (n) the top part of something

telegram (n) a message sent using electricity or radio and then printed and delivered at the other end

thermometer (n) an instrument that measures temperature

vanquish (v) to beat someone in a fight or competition

virgin (n) someone who has never had sex

viscount (n) a man with a title which gives him a high social position; his wife is a **viscountess**